T0106144

Beyond Remembrance

A Haunting Love Story

Dan Hoffman

iUniverse, Inc.
New York   Bloomington

Beyond Remembrance
A Haunting Love Story

iUniverse books may be ordered through booksellers or by contacting:

*iUniverse
1663 Liberty Drive
Bloomington, IN 47403
www.iuniverse.com
1-800-Authors (1-800-288-4677)*

*Because of the dynamic nature of the Internet, any Web addresses or
links contained in this book may have changed since publication and may
no longer be valid. The views expressed in this work are solely those of
the author and do not necessarily reflect the views of the publisher, and
the publisher hereby disclaims any responsibility for them.*

*ISBN: 978-1-4502-4369-8 (sc)
ISBN: 978-1-4502-4370-4 (ebk)*

Printed in the United States of America

iUniverse rev. date: 7/15/2010

DEDICATION

This story primarily is a work of fiction, however its locale and many of the characters written herein are based on my experiences and fond memories gathered over ten years during which time I taught a marine biology course in the British Virgin Islands. I dedicate this novel to the people of Virgin Gorda, and especially to my wife, Marcia the love of my life.

I

Three score and ten years: a span of time that supposedly marks the average human life span. But my dad died when he was not yet seventy-three years old. So he beat the odds by almost three years. My mom outlived him by eight years. She got her four score years in. I thought that I was ready to call it a day when I had just celebrated my sixty fifth birthday, almost four years ago when my heart started acting up. I had only just been retired from my faculty position in the biology department at the university when I suddenly started to experience sudden severe bouts of vertigo. I told the doctors at the hospital, it was like I was plummeting down a steep roller coaster, without any brakes. Atrial fibrillations, they called it. My heart was beating lickety-split out of whack; anywhere from one hundred and seventy plus beats per minute, down to less than thirty. I still had Annie with me then. We had just celebrated our fortieth wedding anniversary and were getting ready to take a cruise up to Alaska. Instead we spent most of the month of June in and out of the local hospital's emergency room and the step-down unit of the intensive care unit. I finally got a pacemaker implant that kept my heart beating normally, at least fifty to sixty beats per minute. A regimen of three prescription drugs taken twice a day kept my heart beat from going into the stratosphere. Of course, then I was also given a prescription for a blood thinner, coumadin, or, as it is known by exterminators, Warfarin or rat poison. The doctors at the hospital informed me since my heart was beating erratically, the blood flow through my vessels was sluggish and could result in the formation of blood clots. That meant that I was prone to getting a stroke. After adjusting my daily dose of this potentially toxic medication, I had to get blood clotting time checked weekly, that is, a measure of the thinness of my blood. After several months of being poked and prodded, my arms had enough puncture wounds in them to rival that of an urban junkie.

Just when I was becoming accustomed to taking enough medication to control, not only my heart rate, but also my blood pressure, enlarged prostate and high cholesterol level, Annie was diagnosed with ovarian cancer. There were no pills that she could swallow that could help her to overcome that damnable disease. Within six months, we celebrated her life at the local church where we worshiped for the past few decades. I suppose it was a beautiful funeral, as one of her friends whispered in my ear at the cemetery. I honored her last wish that her body be cremated. I didn't like the idea that her body that gave me so much pleasure and love over the years of our marriage would be pumped full of preservative chemicals, then placed in a steel casket so that people could gawk at her. We buried her ashes in a silver urn. The grave plot was big enough for at least six such sized containers. The gravesite only had to be large enough to accommodate one more urn when I eventually would pass on.

So it's been almost two years since she left me. For the first two months, I visited her almost every day. I knew that she really wasn't there. Our faith told us that she now lived forever, a new life, where one day hopefully I would join her. But I missed her so damned much. She should have had at least eight more years, if you hold to an average three score and ten year life span. We did return a few months before she left me for a week in Hawaii where we had spent a blissful two weeks on our honeymoon, oh, so many years ago. It was there that our eldest son, Griffin, was conceived. I jokingly wanted to name him Kamehameha, but Annie would have nothing to do with that. Instead we christened him Griffin Louis, his middle name honoring my father.

Five years later, our daughter, Martha Gail, entered our life and completed our family. By then I had taken a faculty position at a small liberal arts college in central Pennsylvania and Annie, having graduated with a degree in management from Seattle University, took a job with the finance office. My doctorate degree was granted to me in Zoology from the University of Washington in Seattle. I met Annie by chance when I was having lunch at the coffee shop at Frederick and Nelson's, a large department store in downtown Seattle. At that time, I was in graduate school, not much money to my name, but enough for a salad and a small Coke. It was love at first sight for me. It took Annie a few more months to realize that I was the right guy for her.

So here I am, four months from reaching the grand old age of seventy years. My son is CEO of a successful electronic engineering firm. He and his family, a wife and three children, have lived in San Francisco for the past fifteen years. Our daughter, Marty, decided to go the route of art school. She and her talented artist husband, Bruce Clapsaddle, both share a faculty position in the art department at Haverford College. My parents didn't give me any siblings to bond with, but my Annie has a brother and a sister who live in California, not too far away from Grif's home in the Bay Area. I'm supposed to celebrate my big seven-zero birthday with my son and his family. They want me to move out there where they can keep their eyes on me. Perhaps I'll go for a week or so. I did say perhaps, didn't I?

It's mid-February in Central Pennsylvania, a dismal, miserably wet, cold time of the year. Before I retired I used to teach an undergraduate marine biology course in the Virgin Islands every June. I knew that I could survive the winter doldrums since it would soon be June, time to head south to the islands. That course initially was to be taught once in a while, but ended up going strong for over twenty years. I'm sitting here now in my office in what was Annie's and my big house going over the ton of photographs we took of the students and our kids enjoying the white sand beaches and the colorful coral reefs. I promised Annie that we'd mount them all in albums, after I retired. So much for good intentions. Perhaps if she hadn't become sick and died....

Right now, I'm trying to decide if I want to spend the rest of my life living by myself. Should I move to San Francisco and pester the hell out of my son and his family? I dearly love my three grandkids, but I need something more than becoming a drag on my son and his family. Annie used to tell me that if we had ever moved to California, because I love to drink good wine, that I would quickly become an alcoholic in no time. God, I miss her so much. Our king sized bed is the loneliest place in town.

Lately I had been falling asleep in front of the television in the family room with our Australian terrier pup, Tillie, snuggling in my lap. She was almost fifteen years old and was starting to have her own set of medical problems. I knew that she would leave me before too long as well. The vet finally told me that Tillie had developed Lupus, an autoimmune disease that caused her to develop smelly sores over her extremities, as well as within her internal organs. There were nights when I could hear her whimper in pain. She used to sleep with us, but the disease caused her to be incontinent, so she had to be relegated to an open kennel that I kept in our bedroom. But I could still hear her crying during the night, partly in pain from the insidious disease that was eating away at her, but also from the pain of separation by not being allowed to share my bed. So I relented and allowed the vet to inject her with steroids that would reduce the pain from her sores and I finally would take her on my lap at night, where we would sleep together in front of the television set. Some mornings there would be a wet spot on my lap since she couldn't hold it anymore. She would look at me with those big, sad, brown eyes apologizing to me for the mess she made. I knew that some would think me cruel for not putting her down, but at the moment, she was all that I had of my old life when Annie and I would snuggle in bed with her.

Finally, one morning when I awoke from sleeping in the lounge chair, I discovered that Tillie had finally left me during the night, eternally asleep in my lap. She looked so tranquil and was finally at peace. She left no wet spot in my lap, but my eyes were full of tears that flowed down and wetted my cheeks for my dear and faithful companion. Now I was truly alone.

Although it was illegal to do so, I buried her ashes, which were contained in a very small, enamel coated tin box, in our grave plot one early evening. I didn't have to dig much of a hole or disturb the grass on the grave site very much. But my two girls finally rest next to one another for all eternity. "Go home, Tillie. Go to Mommy," sobbing, I called out to her after I interred her remains. Looking up to heaven, I prayed to Our Lord to protect these two dearest companions of mine who gave me so much love and pleasure over the years we shared together.

II

Two weeks after Tillie had left me, our valley was inundated by ten inches of heavy, wet snow, brought to us by one of our regular nor'easter storms that often move up the coast during the winter months. Since it occurred on President's Day, the newspapers reported it as Abe and George's storm. That very day my mail contained a brochure extolling the glories of the British Virgin Islands. Then and there I decided to make plans to spend at least the month of March at one of my favorite haunts on Virgin Gorda, one of the more beautiful of the British Virgin Islands. I sent an e-mail to Tina Gottsheid, who is the manager-owner of the Guavaberry-Spring Bay Vacation homes, to see if I could get some accommodations on the island for the month. She responded by days end to inform me that she could fit me in, if I didn't mind spending the first half of the month in one cottage and then moving to another for the rest of my stay. She also told me that the Guavaberry gang was happy to have me return to the island after a five-year absence.

Next I got online and made airline reservations leaving the first weekend of March through Philadelphia to San Juan where I could link up to a connecting flight that would take me to the Beef Island airport that was connected by a causeway to Tortola, the largest of the BVI. From there I could catch a ferry to Virgin Gorda. I completed my round trip plans by returning on the 29th of March, not quite a month, but near enough.

When I called my daughter, Marty, telling her of my plans to spend sometime in the islands, she immediately wanted to join me, for at least the last week of my holiday. She told me that she and her husband, Bruce Clapsaddle, had been planning a trip during the week of spring break. They thought that a week in the islands would be just perfect. I really didn't want to share my holiday with family members. I was looking forward to being on my own. I had just begun working on my sixth novel and I wanted some free time to finish it with my laptop computer.

To digress, I like Bruce, but that name, Clapsaddle, always threw me for a loop. He told me that it was an "old British name that went back to Norman times." I just hated to think of future grandchildren being stuck with such a moniker.

I hadn't been back to the islands in almost five years. I remember the last time I took Annie with me, along with a class of twenty undergraduate students, plus my brother-in-law, Tony Griffin, his wife and two young sons. I told Tony that I would pay for their housing and give him a modest per-diem, paid through the university, if he would help chauffeur the students around in one of the eight passenger trucks we usually rented while in the islands.

Back then we would spend the first half of the course, approximately eight days, on St. John in the American Virgins. For many years, we had rented accommodations and were welcomed by the staff of Cinnamon Bay Campground to their concrete block cottages, just up from one of the most pristine, white sand beaches in the Caribbean. They were basic accommodations, one step up from the canvas tents that also made up a good part of the campground. I liked them for they had electric outlets, ceiling fans and comfortable beds. Annie didn't mind the extrinsic washrooms since they came with flush toilets, lavatories and cold-water showers. Also she knew that, at the end of our stay, we would be moving up to superior accommodations for a week's stay in the Guavaberry cottages on Virgin Gorda that came with all the conveniences of home (full kitchen, hot water showers, etc.), except for air conditioning, which we really didn't miss since the cottages were perched on the side of a hill that was open to the cooling breeze that came off the Caribbean Sea.

But, of course, Annie would not be accompanying me to the islands this year. I knew that once I arrived there, all the old memories of past trips that we took together would begin to haunt me. I didn't know if I would be able to handle it. But I didn't have a choice in the matter, since I had made up my mind that I would be going by myself, at least for the first three weeks.

On departure day I had already notified my good neighbors, the Hobarts, that my home would be vacant for the month of March. I made arrangements with Shawn, who plows my driveway, to take care of any heavy snow that arrived during my absence. I stopped the mail at the post office. I notified my creditors that I would be gone and I would take care of any monthly payments with my computer. I didn't like the idea of giving them access to my bank account, but I didn't want to fall in arrears with my monthly payments to my utility and credit card accounts.

I left the day before I was to fly to the islands to spend the night with the Clapsaddles who were living in a big house outside of Wayne, Pennsylvania. Marty offered to drive me to the airport so that I could catch my early flight out the next morning. She told me that I could park my car, for the duration of my holiday, along their driveway, keeping it safe from the heavy street traffic on Lancaster Boulevard.

Before leaving my home, I decided to pack as little as possible. I would need my computer, which I could carry onto the plane. But the rest of my clothes, my old straw hat, beach clogs and fins were stuffed in my old blue duffel bag that I had used on every trip I had taken in the past to the islands. Along with my computer and a new digital camera, I had to make room for all my medications, something I didn't have to deal with in past years trips. I picked up two mystery novels to read while on a buying trip to Barnes and Nobles. I figured that I would have plenty of time to catch up on my long reading list.

I remembered that on my first trip to Virgin Gorda, I had stopped in one of the harbor shops and innocently asked the manager the inane question: "What do people do for excitement on the island?" He looked at me, smiled and replied, "Why, they listen to the rocks crack." I knew then that I would have plenty of time to catch up on my reading.

Of course, Marty was concerned that I would be "all by myself". "What would you do if some emergency would arise? If you were to get sick again," she asked me while we were enjoying a fine dinner at one of their local restaurants.

"I don't plan on getting sick," I told her as I wound a long string of spaghetti on my dinner fork.

She just sighed. "Well, we'll be down there in three weeks. It just so happens that spring break at the college comes a bit later this year, so it all works out well for us."

I ordered another glass of their fine merlot and looked deeply into my daughter's beautiful, hazel eyes, oh, so like her mothers. "I've been taking care of myself for quite some time now. I think that I can handle a three-week hiatus from civilization."

"But won't you get lonely down there all by yourself?" said Bruce, who stopped munching on a piece of garlic bread to join the conversation.

"At first, I probably will get a bit lonely, but I have made some friends on Virgin Gorda. I'm not taking up the life of a hermit, but I truly am looking forward to and will enjoy the tranquility of sitting on the deck of my cottage with a rum punch in hand, reveling in the beautiful vista before me, each evening as the sun begins to set over the island chain that was first discovered and named by Columbus over five hundred years ago."

When we returned to their home, Marty pulled out one of her photo albums that held hundreds of photographs that she took when she accompanied me on one of my past field trips with my class of students. She had taken the course for credit the summer she graduated from the local high school. Fortunately my colleague, who began to co-teach the course with me when the enrollment began to skyrocket beyond my capacity to handle it, was able to evaluate her work and graded her final field research report.

We spent over an hour or so reminiscing about the good and frantic times we shared that summer. "Do you remember that dog that would follow us into town from our cottages at Guavaberry, Dad? He had the craziest name. Humpy," she began to laugh and tears soon appeared in her eyes. "I remember Mom thought it was an appropriate name for him; he had a difficult time keeping off the other dogs that appeared to reside at the resort."

I decided to change the subject. Looking up at the large painting over the fireplace, I asked her, "Did you paint that landscape from memory? Isn't it the view of the islands from the deck of Hibiscus cottage at Guavaberry?"

"I used one of the photos that I took one early evening, Dad. But most of it came from what I remembered of that beautiful view."

"You can see why I want to return, Marty," I told her as I reached over and took her right hand in mine. "And I'm happy that you and Bruce will be joining me down there. It will bring us closer to your mother, for I know that she loved the islands as well."

Early the following morning after I downed a quick cup of coffee and a glass of orange juice, Marty and Bruce drove me in their new Honda to the Philadelphia airport. I insisted that they just drop me off at the departure lane. I thought it would be foolish to spend money to park the car in the large airport garage since they really couldn't see me off at the gate due to the strict security system that was a result of the 9-ll terrorist attack. I gave my daughter a big hung and kiss on the cheek while Bruce took my duffel bag out of the trunk and placed it on the walkway.

"I really hate to see you going all by yourself, Daddy," she said as she hugged me back, holding back her tears. I told her that I'd be all right and would call her later that evening after I had arrived at my destination. Bruce firmly shook my hand and reminded me that he would see me in a few weeks. "Have a good time, and don't get into any trouble," he jokingly told me as I smiled and waved goodbye to them over my shoulder.

After checking in my bag and receiving my boarding passes, I headed toward the security clearance area before I could reach my departure gate. The line wasn't as long as I had expected. By the time the long queue in which I was standing had reached the screening site, I had to tell them that I wore a pacemaker, so I couldn't pass through the surveillance gateway. One of the security men took me to the side, had me remove my shoes and started to scan my body with an electronic wand. He checked everything. I thought he was going to stick it up my ass after he made a curiously interesting inspection of my genital area. I felt like telling him that I'd never carry any explosives so close to my privates, but I knew better than to say anything that would get me into trouble. Finally I collected my laptop and carry-on bag that held my medication, camera and my favorite plastic Mr. Donut coffee mug that I had taken with me on all my field trips to the islands. I also had packed an extra swimsuit and my facemask and snorkel, just in case my duffel somehow lost its way to the Caribbean. I had learned from past experience that sometimes bags do have a way of arriving a day or two late at your destination.

We boarded the plane twenty minutes before it was to depart for San Juan, Puerto Rico at eight o'clock and, after taking my aisle seat; I found that the middle seat would remain unclaimed. This gave me and the man who was seated in the window seat a bit more room for the three and a half hour flight. The flight down was uneventful. I started to read one of the mystery novels that I had packed, but started to doze off after twenty minutes.

"Oh, Dan, I forgot to call Mrs. Truesdale about the extra house key she'll need in house-sitting Tillie," said Annie who was sitting beside me in the middle seat of Row 12.

I looked at her. She was dressed casually for a trip to the islands wearing a pair of snug fitting blue jeans and a turquoise colored polo shirt. She had just had her naturally curly, gray-streaked,honey blond hair cut short at her favorite stylist so she wouldn't have to put extra time in caring for her hair after she returned from the beach. She looked absolutely beautiful for a woman in her early forties.

"I took care of that, Sweetie, before we left home yesterday. I wanted to be certain that she could get into the house and leave Tillie out for her constitutional. I'm happy that she decided to spend her nights at the house in our guest bedroom. You know Tillie. She has to sleep with someone and Betsy Truesdale loves Tillie and will welcome her as a bedmate."

"I'm happy that Marty has decided to come along with us this year. I think that she'll really enjoy taking your course. I remember when Grif came down with you. He told me that

he had a great time the June after high school graduation, two months before he started his freshman year at Villanova."

"That was the summer that Ted Mitchell started to co-teach the course with me. It was about the only way Grif could have taken the course for credit since I couldn't teach my own son and fairly evaluate his performance for a grade in the course."

"Has it been five years since I've been down to the islands with you? It seems that the only time that I've been able to come down here with you is when one of the kids is taking the course for credit. Either we should have had another child or two, or this might be the last time that I'll be able to come down with you," said Annie, as she reached over to me and held my hand.

"You know that you can come down to the islands anytime you want. I usually come to miss my skinny dipping partner as soon as I get down here," I said as I lifted her hand to my face and kissed it.

"I knew that's all you want from me," she started to laugh and her hazel green eyes sparkled. "I become your sex slave once we get to the islands."

I turned and called the attractive, bosomy flight attendant over and ordered two small bottles of champagne. When she brought them, I paid her the six dollars for the wine, opened them and filled two of the plastic glasses, handing one to Annie.

"You're right, kid, but I tend to be more the sex slave when it comes to you," I said as I raised my glass in a toast. "Here's to you, kid, the true love of my life."

Annie took a sip of champagne and started to laugh. "I remember the last time I was down in the islands with you we almost got caught swimming naked by some of your *students. I didn't realize since there was no moon that night that we had pick that part of the beach where some of the students regularly made out and then went for a swim to cool their jets."*

"Yeh, I don't think that they realized who else took part in their bare assed swimming party that night. Fortunately, they didn't discover us. We had to wait for over an hour, water up to our necks, until they finally got dressed and left the beach, before we could run up to the life guard's chair where we had left our towels and swimsuits." I started to laugh at the situation we had found ourselves in. "We're going to have to be a bit more careful where and when we decide to skinny dip this year."

Annie leaned over to me and kissed me on the lips. "I love you, my crazy darling, Dan."

I awoke from a deep sleep to find that the plane had started to descend, in preparation for its landing at the San Juan airport. I had slept most, if not all of the way to Puerto Rico. Strange, I thought. I hadn't dreamt of Annie for some time.

I checked my itinerary to find that my connecting flight to Beef Island-Tortola was scheduled to leave in fifty minutes. That would give me plenty of time to check out the restroom and visit the Starbuck's stand for a cup of decaf coffee. While I was at it, I also bought a pound of ground decaf coffee that I could enjoy for breakfast while in the islands. Checking the departure monitor, I discovered that my flight to Tortola was scheduled to leave from a gate at the opposite end of the terminal. Good thing I was wearing my new pair of running shoes. I made it with ten minutes to spare.

The flight to the BVI took just over thirty minutes. I had my passport already in hand as I stepped off the plane at the Beef Island airport. After picking up my duffel off the luggage carousel, I headed in the direction of BVI immigration. A willowy, island lady standing behind a large desk asked me if I had anything to declare. I had filled out the immigration form on the plane and handed it to her with my passport. After she scribbled on the form, she stamped my passport and told me to have an enjoyable holiday in the British Virgin Islands. Now how much smoother could that have been?

She told me that there was a Speedy's passenger ferry ready to leave the airport dock for Virgin Gorda. The next ferry would not leave for another two hours. In just over a half an hour I would find myself back at my old haunts at Guavaberry. I boarded the ferry, throwing my duffel bag with the others on the stern of the ship; then I paid the ten-dollar transport fee to the purser and took a seat on the upper deck of the ferry. Taking off my jacket, I could feel the warm sun on my bare arms. I took my sunglasses out of my coat pocket, put them on, and leaning back in the seat, enjoyed the warm tropical sun on my face. It felt great to be back. I delighted at the beautiful azure blue water that the ferry smoothly cut through on its way to the island. I just wished that Annie could share all of this with me. I kept thinking about the dream I had while asleep on the plane. It seemed so real, as if she was really coming down to the islands with me.

III

The ferry pulled up to the concrete dock at Virgin Gorda and the crew quickly began to unload the passenger's baggage. I stepped down onto the dock and realized that it had been almost five years since I had last done so. Usually, in past years, I would be in charge of a retinue of excited undergraduate students, but this was a first for me, to be on my own. I picked up my duffel and carry-on bag that contained by lap top computer, medication and an assortment of other necessities and headed up the dock. Since I had already cleared for entry into the BVI through customs at the airport on Beef Island, I did not have to wait in line to be cleared for entry as I had done over the years with my students.

As in my past visits to the island, there were a number of taxis waiting to pick up fares to take them to wherever they wished to go on the island. I had not made arrangements with Tina to reserve a car for me, but I quickly found out that there was a representative from Mahogany Car Rentals already there with a small car for me. Tina had anticipated that I would likely want to rent one, and she was right again. The transaction went quickly. I showed them my Pennsylvania driver's license, paid the ten dollars for the temporary license and was handed the keys to a late model Jeep.

Although there was no town as such on Virgin Gorda, there was a settlement at the west end of the island called Spanishtown. There was also a small shopping center made up of a dozen or more venues that served the large yacht harbor basin that was originally developed by the Rockefeller Foundation to promote yachting in the islands. I drove into the parking lot of the center remembering to keep to the left side of the road. I thought that I'd pick up some provisions for I had planned to prepare my own meals; at least for the first few days I was in the islands. I remembered that Buck's Super Market had moved to the Little Dix Bay Commissary a few years before I stopped coming to the islands. Within twenty minutes I had picked up enough foodstuffs, a six pack of Diet Coke and a bottle of Mount Gay rum to satisfy my needs, at least until I made another foray to the market.

It's about a mile and a half to the Guavaberry resort, on the road past the island school, to the main tourist attraction on the island. The Baths are now part of the British Virgin Islands National Park System. The island has an interesting geological history where, millions of years ago, huge, monolithic granite boulders were spewed up from the bowels of the earth by volcanic action littering the landscape and the coastal beaches. Some of the boulders reach heights of over twenty feet. They form interesting arrangements of rocks that frame pools of water that resemble shallow bath tubs. A quarter of a mile from the entrance to The Baths I came to the right turn off at the Guavaberry-Spring Bay Vacation Homes sign. I soon discovered that the resort had built a new office complex that contained a game room with high-speed Internet access. It was a concrete structure with three roof peaks and a planting of red ixora and yellow alamanda that beautifully framed its front face. The only phone at the resort was also located in the complex. I liked the isolation of not having a telephone in my cottage. Upon opening the door I was greeted by Valerie, an associate of the resort and a good friend.

"It's wonderful having you back at Guavaberry, Dan," she said as her eyes smiled back at me. "This time you're not surrounded by your large class of students."

"Yes, I decided to go it alone. I had to find time to re-discover the beauty and tranquility of the island."

"I thought you'd be bringing Annie with you," she asked.

"Annie passed away two years ago."

"Oh, I'm sorry," she began to apologize, I didn't realize that…."

I interrupted her. "My daughter and son-in-law will be joining me toward the end of my stay here. Plus I brought my lap top computer. I'm working on a new novel and hope to complete it before I leaving the islands."

"I enjoyed reading your last two novels. I took them with me when I vacationed on Anegada last year. So I'll be looking forward to your new novel when it is published."

"Where's Tina? I wanted to thank her for remembering to rent me a vehicle from Mahogany? Does Puck still run the car rental agency?"

"Tina had to run to the settlement and will be back in an hour or so. And Puck does still operate the vehicle rental agency."

"Well, my next question is where are my digs for the duration?"

"We put you in a one-bedroom cottage just south of Hibiscus for the next three weeks. After your family members join you, you'll be back in the two-bedroom unit, Hibiscus. I know that it is your favorite of all our cottages, especially with its beautiful view of the islands." She reached to the keyboard behind her desk and removed a set of keys. "Here are the keys to Lily cottage. I think you'll enjoy the southern view of the Caribbean from its deck."

After asking her to give my regards to Tina and her husband, Ludwig, I returned to my car and headed across the highway, through the gateway with its tubular metal cattle guard, and up the narrow drive, between the boulder field that was surrounded by flowering tropical shrubs and trees. At the traffic circle in front of Plum and Jasmine cottages, I headed the car past the elevated octagonal cottages to my own island hide-a-way with its spectacular view of the Caribbean. I started to realize that I was here by myself, and began to feel melancholy that I had no one to share this wonderful experience with.

I had never stayed in Lily cottage before since it had but one bedroom. Five years ago, two gay men had been sharing the cottage while Annie and I were sharing the two-bedroom Hibiscus cottage with Grif and his wife, Sophie. I grabbed my duffel and carry-on bag and climbed the staircase to the umber painted wooden deck of the cottage. I looked around and was excited to be able to see

Tortola and Mt. Sage on the eastern horizon. Unlocking the door, I stepped into the cottage. I had a sudden sense of deja vu. The common room of kitchen-dining and living room resembled that of Hibiscus, down to the wicker furniture and the container of red hibiscus blossoms on the table. Even the smell of the cottage seemed the same. I entered the bedroom to find a single queen size bed covered with a tropical motif coverlet. Again I wished that Annie were with me. I started to have doubts that I would be able to spend three weeks by myself in this beautiful, tranquil place. I decided to get down to business and started to unpack my belongings in an attempt to turn my thoughts to happier times. Then I remembered that I had left the groceries in the trunk of the car, so I headed down the stairs and removed the bags of foodstuffs. I placed the bag of Starbuck's coffee that I bought in San Juan next to the coffee maker, and put the dry goods in the cabinet over the stove and the eggs, milk and chicken breasts that I would bake for dinner that night in the refrigerator-along with the six pack of soda.

I opened the bottle of Mount Gay rum, filled a glass with ice cubes from the freezer tray and topped the glass off with some of the cola from an open can. Traditionally, on past trips, whenever we first arrived and settled in at one of the Guavaberry cottages, I would make myself a drink and also for whomever else accompanied me, be it Annie, Ted or my brother-in-law, Tony; and it was always rum and cokes made with Mount Gay rum. We'd move to the deck with drinks in hand and sit in the canvas-backed directors chairs around the table and take in the view of the islands. We then knew that we had finally arrived on Virgin Gorda.

The sun was beginning to set over Beef Island. The hottest part of the day was coming to an end. In another hour or so it would be twilight, the start of my first evening in the Caribbean in many years. There was a moderating cooling breeze coming in from the south, off the Caribbean. There would be good sleeping weather tonight. I had remembered to bring my small portable radio-cassette player with me to keep me in tune with the world. I checked the bottom of my bag to find that I did pack several Jimmy Buffett tapes. It seems that Jimmy had kept me company on most of my field trips to the islands, and tonight would be no exception.

As I walked into the kitchen and replenished my drink, a small car drove up to my cottage. It was Tina coming to say hello.

"Ahoy, there, Tina!" I called out to her. "Thank you for remembering to rent a Jeep for me. It was something that I entirely forgot to have you do for me."

"You usually requested vehicles. I figured that if you didn't want one you could always have cancelled it on your arrival. Better safe than sorry. It's good to have you with us again, Dan. Valerie told me about Annie's passing. My sympathy to you."

"Thank you, but please let's not discuss her now. I just want to enjoy the great ambiance of this wonderful place you call home."

"I see you're with us for a month this time."

"Yes, I'll be here by myself for the first three weeks, but my daughter, Marty and her husband, Bruce will be joining me for the last week."

"I remember when she was down here, when was it ten years ago?"

"Actually it was more than fifteen. She is an art professor now at Haverford College where her husband is also a member of the faculty."

"Has it really been that long, Dan?" she replied.

"I'm afraid so. I'll be turning the big seven-zero this summer."

"Well, don't turn into a hermit while you're here. Ludwig and I must take you over to Saba Rock Resort for dinner sometime next week. I'll be in touch. Please feel free to use the Internet service we now have in our office."

"Oh, I shall. It's good seeing you, again; my best to Ludwig and your daughter, Michelle."

After Tina drove off, I decided to make myself a light supper. I grilled one of the chicken breasts, which I had marinated in lime juice, garlic and olive oil. The piece of grilled chicken and a small salad with a vinagrette dressing was more than enough supper for me that first evening on the island. With the radio tuned to my favorite St. Croix station that played the oldies from the sixties and seventies each evening, I cleaned up my dishes and headed out onto the deck. For the next hour so I just enjoyed the view across the Sir Francis Drake Channel. The lights were beginning to be turned on all over Tortola. They sparkled and twinkled almost like they were part of some mystical Oz-like fairyland across the sea. The airport beacon atop Beef Island started to wink on and off. I used to tell Annie that I swore there was more than one beacon atop that mountain, for if you focused long enough on that blinking light, there appeared to be at least two of them up there.

By nine o'clock I was starting to feel the effects of a long day of traveling. I remembered my promise to call Marty on my arrival, but I didn't feel like walking down to the resort office to use the phone. I promised myself that I would call her first thing in the morning on my way to Spring Bay beach for my first swim of the day.

After brushing my teeth and relieving myself of the rum punches I had drunk, I decided to call it a night. I threw my clothes across a chair in the bedroom and crawled under the bed sheet. There was a soft warm breeze entering the room through the jalousie windows so I decided to turn off the ceiling fan. I don't remember falling asleep.

"Why did you turn off the fan, Dan? You know it keeps the mosquitoes from pestering us while we sleep," said Annie as she crawled into bed along side of me. She was wearing only the tops of her shorty pajamas that she had been packing in her suitcase for the islands the past few years.

She reached under the bed covers and began to stroke my belly. "Interested in a little nocturnal recreation, Sweetie?" She coyly said as she began to nibble on my left ear lobe.

I could feel my member becoming hard as her hand slid further down and began to play with the curly pubic hair that surrounded my genitals. "Oh, my!" she softy exclaimed." It looks like it didn't take you all that long to get in the mood."

Annie sat up in bed and pulled her pajama tops over her head, exposing her firm breasts. The phosphorescent light entering through the window from the full moon highlighted her rosy nipples. Moving back under the covers, she began to move her hands over my body, finally coming to rest on my member. I pulled her on top of me and began to massage her ample breasts, while she kissed me deeply on the mouth. I found myself entering her as she began to move up and down over my body. We would never speak a word during our lovemaking for a long as I could remember. Soon I could feel the tension of release in both of our bodies. We both cried out in unison as we reach the climax of our lovemaking.

She lay atop me for several minutes while we exchanged kisses. Then she slid off me and looking deeply into my eyes began to smile. "I love you, my dearest one," she said as she drifted off to sleep.

"I'll always love you, my darling."

IV

When I awoke a half hour later, it was still not eleven o'clock by the luminous dials on my dive watch. Had I really been dreaming? Annie's presence seemed so real. I felt that she was present in the bedroom, yet I knew that I did lose her over two years ago. I arose from the bed and decided to take a warm shower. Afterward, I put on a pair of gym shorts and went out onto the deck and looked up at the tropical night sky that was filled with countless stars. I began to shake. Was I going mad? Had she really come to me while I slept?

The crowing of feral roosters awoke me before the sun had risen. A gray morning light filled the bedroom. Although I had slept most of the night I still felt tired. The dream that I experience the night before still haunted me. Somehow I started to feel that Annie's spirit was with me on this holiday.

The day lay before me. I had no definite plans or schedule for my daytime activities. I remembered that I had to call Marty for I knew that she would be worrying if I didn't do so. Somehow I dozed off for another hour or so. When I awoke, I heard the birds chirping in the trees. I padded barefoot into the kitchen and put some ground coffee into the percolator after I half filled it with water from the tap. After a quick trip to the bathroom to use the toilet and brush my teeth, I put on my new pair of swim trunks, an old, faded tee shirt that I had bought in the islands several years past, and a pair of beach-tongs. I was ready for the day. I've never been much for breakfast. I poured myself a cup of coffee and cut a slice from a loaf of banana bread that I bought in town, lathering it with rich Danish butter. I almost forgot to take my regimen of medication, in all eight pills and capsules, downed with some of the cola that was left over from the night before.

I took the coffee and the bread out onto the deck, where I sat at the table enjoying the early morning view of the distant islands. To the left of Tortola, I could make out the outline of St. John. It couldn't be more than fifteen miles distant, if that much. After I finished my light breakfast, I put on my sunglasses and grabbed a beach towel from the closet and headed down the driveway to the office on the other side of the main highway.

I found the telephone and quickly dialed Marty's number charging the call to my Visa card. Luck would have it that Marty still had not left for her classes at the University. There was an hour difference between us. The Virgin Islands were on Atlantic Time, an hour ahead of the U.S. Eastern Seaboard. She was relieved that I had called. She told me that she was starting to get worried last night since I had not called her to tell her that I had arrived. I felt like she was taking over the responsibility from her mother, since I usually had to call Annie whenever I was out of town attending a meeting or presenting a paper at a convention.

"It's a beautiful morning in the islands, Marty. I'm on my way down to Spring Bay for my first swim of the day."

"Be careful, daddy. You're all by yourself. Don't swim out too far."

"Yes, mother," I joshed her. I told her that I loved her and would call again in the next few days."

After hanging up the phone, I wrote my name and time of call in the register by the phone. Each call was assessed a dollar by the Guavaberry resort. I then headed down the path between the beach houses that fronted on the bay. When I arrived at the beach I found that I was the only one there, except for two of the local dogs that were romping in the sand. Other than a small surf action on the edge of the powder sand beach, the surface of the water appeared as smooth as glass. I quickly kicked off my beach flip-flops and placed the towel with my glasses in a beach chair and headed toward the water. It was the first time that I had visited Virgin Gorda in the springtime. Usually we would arrive with our classes in mid June for a week's stay. I quickly discovered that the water was not quite as warm as it was in June, for there was a slight chill to it. But after a few minutes, I adjusted to the temperature difference and began to swim laps up and down the beach.

After swimming for twenty minutes, I left the water and trotted up to the beach chair, draping the towel over my shoulder and placing the sunglasses over my eyes. I soon discovered that I no longer had the beach to myself.

A tall willowy woman dressed in a skimpy yellow and red bikini swimsuit was walking down the beach toward me. I was quick to notice that she amply filled the swimsuit. She cut quite a striking figure with short cropped, blond hair and a deep tanned body. I decided not to continue to stare at her as she approached me. Instead I turned and began to watch a finely rigged sloop off shore as it sailed southward, probably heading toward The Baths.

"Here I thought I would have the beach all to myself," said the woman to me as I turned and looked into her green eyes. I was surprised that she was wearing so little for so early in the morning.

"I'm sorry to disturb your solitude," I replied as I stood from the chair.

"When did you arrive? I know most of the people who spend any time on this beach," she replied in turn.

I noticed that she was barefoot and her toenails, as well as her fingernails, were painted an iridescent shade of pink.

"Yesterday afternoon. I'm staying up in one of the Guavaberry cottages. I've been coming down here for years, but usually later in the season, mid June."

"That must be why I don't know you. I go by the name of Tess. And you are….?"

"Oh, how rude of me, I'm Daniel Henderson."

"Please to make your acquaintance, Daniel Henderson. Are you down here with your family?"

"No, I decided to play the hermit and come to the islands by myself this year."

"So you left your family to face the winter weather all by themselves?"

"No, my children are both married and have left home. My wife passed on two years ago."

"An unattached man… interesting," she said as she smiled at me with a mouth filled with teeth that resembled lustrous pearls.

"How about you?" I started to feel an attraction to this island woman.

"What do you want to know, Daniel? Like you, I'm here by myself looking for a little excitement. My husband, well, I don't see much of him anymore. He left me with two children, but I'm fairly well off. Are you looking for a bit of excitement to help pass your time on the island?"

It was then that I noticed the large diamond and sapphire ring that she wore on her right ring finger, as she combed her hand through her short hair.

"I was about to take a dip, but I thought I would have the beach to myself. I don't want to get my new bikini wet. Interested in joining me for a skinny dip? I'll show you mine, if you show me yours."

She started to laugh as she started to untie her bikini tops exposing a pair of evenly tanned, full breasts. "You can see that I usually don't wear anything in the water."

I was starting to feel aroused by this strange woman that I had just met. She slipped off her bottoms exposing a tuft of golden hair.

"Now it's your turn, Danny Boy, she coyly said as she turned and ran into the sea leaving me behind, watching her beautiful shapely buns disappear under the water.

I was grateful that she could not see that I had become hard. I dropped my swim shorts, threw the towel and glasses back on the chair and followed her lead into the sea. I couldn't believe that this was happening to me.

She had swum out about twenty meters and looked back at me and smiled as she saw me treading water toward her. As I came up to her I found that she quickly reached over to me and began to stroke my erect organ.

"You've got quite a hard one there, Danny Boy. You probably haven't had much opportunity to use it lately, have you?" She smiled at me, her green eyes flashing, as she pulled herself against my body.

"Have you ever made love like the fishes, Danny?

I didn't want to tell her that Annie liked to do it while we were swimming nude at night. She reached over to me and continued to fondle me. I had never experienced a woman like Tess before. I was amazed that I had only been on the island for less than a day and I was already behaving like one of my past randy students, allowing this woman to take advantage of me.

She started to laugh as she pulled away from me and began to swim back to the shore. I watched her leave the water and run naked up the beach to where I had left my suit and towel. She quickly picked up the pieces of her bikini, turned and smiled at me and began to run down the beach, retracing her steps. I watched her as she disappeared behind a large boulder field.

I thought to myself. Would I meet this amazing woman again? She made me feel young again. Yet I felt guilty that somehow I was cheating on Annie, even though she had left me two years past.

V

I jogged back to my cottage where I showered and dressed in a blue polo shirt and a white pair of shorts. I slipped my new sandals on my bare feet, put my wallet into my pocket, gathered the car keys, and decided to drive up to The Top of the Baths for lunch. It was just a short drive, probably less than a couple hundred meters to the top of the hill that overlooked the Baths. I remembered when the complex of shops and a fine restaurant with a small fresh water swimming pool first opened. It must have been in the late nineties. I parked the Jeep in the traffic circle along side the large jitney cabs that transported the daily visitors that came for a days stay from other islands just to swim at The Baths.

I found that I was still a bit early for lunch for most of the restaurant tables were unoccupied. I sat under an umbrella that shaded the table. One of the island wait staff took my order for an ice tea and a chicken salad sandwich and left me to enjoy the tranquility of the island scenery that sparkled in the tropical sunlight before me.

My thoughts turned to my early morning encounter with the beautiful woman who aroused long lost passion within me. I had to find out more about this woman, especially where she was living on the island.

Within ten minutes I was joined in the restaurant by several young people. One couple had two young children that had discovered the pool and were soon frolicking and splashing within it.

I had the day to myself. After I had finished my lunch I decided to return to my cottage and spend an hour or so reading one of my new mystery novels. When I arrived at the cottage I was surprised to find a dog curled up and asleep on the deck. It was a golden short-haired "island" dog, a mix of all the canine genes found on the island. From her sleeping position, I could see that the dog was a female. My arrival caused her to lift her head and look at me.

"Hi, Girl, I don't remember seeing you the last time we were here." I reached down and scratched her behind her floppy ear. She almost appeared to smile as she put her head down and continued her siesta. I couldn't help but notice that her paws were wet with sand between her toes. "Just back from the beach, old girl?" I asked her, not expecting her to reply. "Since I don't know your name, I'm gonna call you Sandy. How's that for an appropriate name?" When she seemed to smile, I said, "Sandy it is."

Later in the day, when the sun's heat had diminished somewhat, I decided that I would drive over to Savanna Bay and check out the snorkeling on the fringing reef. When I was involved with the course, my colleague Ted Mitchell and I would use Savanna Bay almost exclusively as a study site for our students. We had twice daily field trips and had the students undertake different quantitative and qualitative studies of the reef tract: vertical transects and ten square meter quadrants in order to study the composition and distribution of the coral and associated reef creatures. It would have been five years since last I had visited the reef tract at the bay. I was beginning to wonder what state of activity or decay I would discover after the many years I had not snorkeled there.

After reading for an hour out on the deck with my canine friend asleep under my chair, I decided that the book could no longer hold my interest. I gathered my snorkeling equipment, pulled up my swim trunks and found another towel in the bathroom. When I approached my rental car, I found my new canine friend waiting for me.

"Want to go for a ride with me, Sandy?"

I opened the back door of the car and she joyfully jumped inside. Obviously she was accustomed to riding in a car. I thought that she had to be someone's pet, most likely Tina's or Valerie's.

The drive took me past St. Ursula's Church built on a promontory that overlooked the yacht basin. It reminded me that the next day would be Sunday and I should attend services, in deference to my wife. She always enjoyed the music and singing at the Mass; old standards hymns sung and played to a calypso beat. Within five minutes I rounded the point that overlooked Savanna Bay. Virgin Gorda was shaped like a figure eight with a narrow isthmus joining them together, over which the main highway from one to the other part of the island passed. The upper section was capped by Gorda Peak with narrow steep roads that wrapped around the mountain, while the lower section was relatively flat and was the most populated region of the island. Savanna Bay formed the northern crux between the two halves. There was a beautiful beach on this leeward side of the island, having little surf action, while on the other side of the isthmus, there was a classical windward beach composed primarily of jagged pieces of volcanic stones and coral rocks on which the turbulent surf broke.

I turned left, followed a dirt road and soon parked under a grove of pepper and cashew trees that afforded the only shade in the bay. From the lack of any other parked cars, I assumed that I had the beach and the reef to myself that afternoon.

After gathering my snorkeling gear, I locked the car and, with Sandy at my side, walked out onto one of the most picturesque beaches in the Caribbean. I was correct in assuming that I would be the only person to enjoy the beach that afternoon. I sat on the sun heated beach sand and put my fins on first, followed by my facemask and snorkel. I had locked my wallet in the Jeep and put the keys in a mesh dive bag along with my towel and shirt. I was eager to enter the water and to begin to explore the reef, but I was certain to apply a coat of sunscreen, especially to my face and on the back of my neck and legs. I decided to wear an old tee shirt to protect my back from the tanning ultraviolet rays of the sun. No good tempting fate. I still have not had any problems with skin cancer after all the years of coming down to the islands.

Sandy ran down the empty beach and disappeared behind a boulder field. It appeared she had been here before.

The afternoon sun had warmed the shallow water of the bay to a temperature that almost approached bathwater. It was very relaxing just to loll and enjoy the sensuous pleasure of swimming in water with crystal clear visibility. My first thought was to swim out a few meters and check the state of the reef. I first noticed that many of the large coral heads appeared to be in bad condition. Some were partially overgrown with a filamentous green alga, while others showed the white spotting disease indicating that the symbiotic algae within the polyps were dead or dying. The sea whips and sea feather gorgonian corals appeared to be in better condition. At least I would see that their polyps were alive and extending from their skeletal framework. As I swam out further, a small school of blue tangs, about fifteen in all, were swimming in tight formation in the distance. I could see them feeding on the algal fuzz that was growing on the coral rock. There was an abundance of the usual assemblage of colorful reef fish: striped damselfish, iridescent parrotfish and curious wrasses that swam and foraged on the reef tract. I counted at least six varieties of each. So far so good, I thought, as far as the diversity of fish was concerned.

After snorkeling over the reef for over an hour, I decided to relax on the beach and enjoy the scenic beauty of the bay. Still alone on the beach I removed my wet trunks and shirt and wrung out most of the water. I was enjoying the freedom of a quick nude sunbath when I heard a car door close in the parking lot. Quickly I pulled up my wet trunks just in the nick of time, as two young couples emerged through the trees and started to walk down the beach toward me. I had the feeling that my presence was cramping their style when I saw a disappointed look on their faces. Presumably they came to the beach either to do some nude swimming or to make out, or possibly both. With that in mind, I picked up my towel and mesh bag and headed back to my car, telling them as I walked past them that the beach was all theirs. I was quick to notice that their faces lit up with broad smiles at hearing the news. My new pal Sandy was waiting for me at the car. I opened the door and she quickly hopped in as if she owned it.

I drove back to the yacht basin shopping center, having put on my polo shirt since I remembered that bare-chested visitors were not welcome anywhere in the islands except on the beaches. When I parked in the lot adjacent to the center, I opened the door and Sandy once again jumped out and ran toward the marina. I figured she was familiar with this area. I locked the car and decided to do some shopping. I picked up some postcards at the dive shop and perused their collection of tee shirts thinking that I might buy some for my grandchildren. However, before I could make up my mind, I became aware that my mysterious swimming partner from earlier that day had just walked past the dive shop windows and appeared to be heading toward the parking lot. She was dressed in a green sundress that complemented her flaxen golden hair. I quickly paid for the postcards and dashed from the shop, but when I reached the parking lot she was nowhere to be seen. Perhaps I would meet her again when next I come into the yacht basin complex.

Upon returning to my Jeep, I discovered that Sandy was waiting for me. "Where'd you go, girl? Ready to go back to the cottage with me?" I opened the car door and she hopped in sitting in the seat beside me.

When I arrived back at my cottage, I decided that I had to discover the identity of this mysterious, sexy lady. After I showered, I dressed in clean clothes and drove down to the Guavaberry office. No doubt, either Tina or Valerie would know something about her identity.

However, when I addressed the issue to them they knew nothing of her identity.

I told them, without going into details, that I had met her on the beach at Spring Bay that morning. They thought that she may have been staying at the resort at Little Dix Bay, but somehow I felt that she was staying in the Guavaberry resort area, perhaps visiting friends who had rented a beach house.

By then, it was late afternoon. I decided to drive back to my cottage and relax before I made myself some supper for that night. It was Saturday night, perhaps I should make the rounds of some of the smaller resorts, or even drive out to the Little Dix Bay resort, but it had been a long day and I decided that tomorrow would be another day to go exploring.

After I cooked and ate the remaining marinated chicken breast and some fresh broccoli, I decided to take out my laptop computer and work on my new novel. I began working on it a few weeks past. I was writing the story of my graduate school experiences at the University of Washington, and especially how I came to know and marry Annie.

I had written to the point where I first met her when I stopped at the small restaurant in the Frederick and Nelson department store in downtown Seattle. I had found a empty table for two near the window facing Fifth Avenue and was about to begin eating a salad, when

Annie came to the table and asked if I would mind if she shared the table with me since all the other tables were occupied. I immediately stood and told her that I would be happy to have her join me for lunch. I was quick to introduce myself and she did likewise.

By the time we had eaten our lunch I had told her that I was a graduate student in the zoology department at the University of Washington, and she informed me that she was a senior finance major at Seattle University. Annie Griffin shared an apartment with two other students on Capitol Hill, although her parents lived in West Seattle. I felt that I had known this vivacious, young woman with the blonde ponytail and the bright hazel green eyes all my life. I couldn't let her go without asking if I could see her again. She must have seen something in me as well, for she asked me if I would like to meet her roommates by coming over for dinner that coming Saturday night. It happened all so fast. Something had clicked. From that moment on, we seemed to be inseparable. I was a third year graduate student who would be starting my residency at the University's marine laboratory at Friday Harbor, on San Juan Island the following summer quarter, having spent the previous two summers at the lab starting my doctoral research on crustacean reproductive endocrinology.

I knew that I would have to move quickly if I didn't want to lose her. Annie graduated with high honors in finance in May and the following month we were married in her parent's Catholic Church. After honeymooning in Hawaii, Annie joined me up at Friday Harbor, telling me the first night as we shared one of the lab's primitive hut-like cottages that she was pregnant with our first child. I had met her initially in early February over lunch and four months later we were not only married, but were pregnant as well.

That summer was…well…oh, so magical for Annie and me! While I was working on my research project, Annie was hired part-time in the lab's main office working with, the director's assistant, Estelle Kraft, on the financial accounts of the laboratory. By the end of the summer, after most of the visiting scientists and postdoctoral candidates had left, we found ourselves moved into one of the recently vacated furnished one-bedroom apartments at Cantilever Point.

Even though, Annie was a few months pregnant with our first child, Griffin, it seemed that we enjoyed each other intimately almost every night until she was in her eight month of pregnancy.

By early March I asked Annie, who was now close to giving birth, to move back to her parent's home in West Seattle, where she would be close to a hospital where she would give birth to our first son. I took two weeks off from my research responsibilities at the labs and accompanied her to her parent's home. Two days after we arrived, I had to rush her to the maternity ward of the hospital where our son Griffin was born.

Two weeks later the three of us took the ferry from Anacortes back to Friday Harbor. For my last summer on the islands, when I was completing my doctoral research and writing my dissertation, we rented a small, rustic cottage a few miles out of town off the American Camp Road where we set up housekeeping and began to raise our young son.

By the end of the autumn quarter, early December, I had completed the first draft of my dissertation and we decided to move back to Seattle, since my reading committee members were in residence at the main campus. To save money, we moved in with Annie's parents and her two younger siblings. Her parents were overjoyed in having their grandson living with them. Annie and I at first felt under scrutiny, but we came to realize that, by the beginning of the summer, I would have defended my dissertation and received my doctorate.

I had been receiving a stipend from the predoctoral fellowship that was granted to me from the National Science Foundation. Back then a monthly stipend of two hundred and sixty seven dollars kept the wolf away from the door. I was still driving my old Plymouth Valiant convertible that seemed to be holding up. With the grandparents and her two siblings offering to babysit our son, Annie took a part time job in the finance office of Seattle University.

While waiting for my committee members to read and pass on my dissertation, I started looking for future employment. At first it appeared that the job market for recent Ph.D.s had dried up. Then one day in early March, I received a telephone call from the chair of the biology department at San Francisco State University. Would I be interested in applying and interviewing for a tenure track position at State? I jumped at the opportunity. However, a week later, I received another call, this time from the dean of the college who informed me that all new faculty positions at the university had been frozen by the California state legislature as an austerity move.

By the end of March I still had no job offer and my dissertation defense was but two months away. My undergraduate advisor at UC Berkeley, Cadet Hand, came to my rescue. He was in touch with the director of the Duke University Marine Laboratory who was also involved with crustacean hormonal research projects. He was looking for someone to take on a project as a postdoctoral candidate for a two-year period. The position was supported through his training grant and would pay the princely sum of six thousand dollars per annum.

I told Annie about the offer and she told me to apply. I would have to be interviewed by the director of the lab, which meant that I would have to travel to the laboratory, which was located near Beaufort, North Carolina, on the southern end of the Outer Bank chain of sea-islands. Never having been east of the Rocky Mountains before, I was a bit apprehensive about taking my family so great a distance from Annie's family in Seattle.

At that time, my parents lived in Santa Rosa, California. We had just visited them with their new grandson over the Christmas holiday. Moving to the Eastern Seaboard would be a major change in our family life. But Annie was positive that I make arrangements to fly to Raleigh where I would be able to rent a car and drive the extra distance to Beaufort.

I still remember Annie driving me to the Sea-Tac airport where I caught a flight through St. Louis to Raleigh. She was my source of strength and more than helped me make the decision to apply for the position at the Duke Lab.

After driving the distance across the flat Carolina Coastal Plain, I arrived with some trepidation at the Duke Lab. How different it appeared from the Friday Harbor Lab! The laboratory buildings were covered with graying cedar shakes and were located on a barren looking island that was connected to the mainland by a short bridge-like causeway. Across the sound, the town of Beaufort appeared like a city out of time. It was also the first time I had experienced Southern hospitality. The director, Dr. John Costlow, a large, affable man who rarely took his pipe from his mouth, took me under his wing and gave me a grand tour of the facilities, which at that time were basic to say the least. They checked me into one of the dormitory rooms that I would be sharing with a recently arrived postdoctoral fellow who at that time was not married. That first evening, the director hosted a big party at is home on Ann Street in Beaufort. He and his gracious wife lived in a white frame, two storied antebellum house. At any moment I expected to see Scarlet O'Hara come sashaying down the curved staircase in a red velvet dress. The director and his wife filled me with fresh local seafood and numerous glasses of wine. By the end of the evening, I had been made welcome by the wonderful hospitality of all the laboratory personnel. I knew where Annie and I would be living come summer.

I had been working at my word processor for well over three hours without stopping for a break. I decided to stop for the evening, made myself a rum-soaked drink and sat out on the deck. It was time to enjoy the tropical night view of the islands. I had recalled all my early memories of Annie, the first few years of our marriage that seemed so idyllic to me. I began to feel very guilty about being "unfaithful" to her with my mystery lady whom I had met and almost had sex with. I poured myself another glass of Mount Gay rum over the rocks and again wished that

Annie were beside me, supporting my work on this new book that I plan to dedicate to her and our children.

Suddenly I didn't feel alone. My new canine companion was waiting for me.

I decided that I would go to church the following morning. I'd forego the early morning swim, just in case my mystery lady would be lying in wait for me. I drained the last of my rum, went into the bathroom, took a leak and brushed my teeth. After turning out the lights in the central room, I headed for my bed and a good nights sleep.

But before I could fall asleep, there came a scratching at the door. Rising from my bed, I opened the door to find Sandy sitting upright on her haunches. She seemed to be smiling. Feeling a bit lonely, I said, "Do you want to come in and sleep inside?"

She trotted in, jumped onto the bed, and took up a position at the foot of my bed, closed her eyes and fell asleep. I fondly remembered how Tillie used to sleep with Annie and me.

VI

Where am I? I find myself in a dimly lighted room. Before me there is a bed within which lies a woman who appears to be dying. I now realize that it is my Annie. Her breathing is shallow and labored. I come to her side and take her hand. She looks up at me with her hazel green eyes; eyes that have lost their radiance. Her face is ashen. What remains of her lustrous hair was covered by a white stocking cap. The terrible chemotherapy treatments that she had endured for the past month have robbed of her silken golden crown.

I take her thin hand in mine and press it to my lips. My eyes are filled with tears.

"Danny, is it really you?" she calls to me with a weak voice. "I knew you'd come. I must leave you my darling, but not for long. Look for me....look for me. I will be waiting for you, my darling , my darling.…."

"I cry out in desperation. "No, no, please, Annie, stay with me, stay with me, my dearest love."

I woke up with a start. My body was drenched in sweat. I felt my heart beating erratically. The night air had turned hot and humid. I had forgotten to turn on the ceiling fan in the bedroom. I got out of bed and put on a pair of boxer shorts and walked barefoot into the kitchen area and poured myself a glass of ice water from the pitcher in the refrigerator and swallowed my prescription medication. I looked at the luminous hands of my watch. It was just past midnight. I had only been sleeping for just under two hours. I opened the door to the cottage and walked out onto the deck and sat in one of the director's chairs by the table. I thought to myself that I was probably primed to experience such a dream after spending a good part of the evening writing about Annie and our early days together in Washington State.

When I returned to the bedroom I discovered that Sandy was no where to be seen. Where did she go? I couldn't remember her following me out onto the deck. Perhaps she did and I didn't notice her leaving

After a quick shower the next morning, I put on a pair of dress slacks and a clean button down shirt and my only red tie. Since it was Sunday, I decided to attend Mass at St. Ursula's. It's an impressive modern designed structure that was built on a promontory that overlooked the yacht harbor. Annie loved to attend Mass there when we stayed on the island since the choir sang such great hymns to the lilting calypso beat of the Caribbean. When we first arrived on Virgin Gorda, we met the pastor, an Irish priest by the name of Father Whyte. He told us the story of how he built the church from contributions he had received from visitors. One couple that had sailed in on a big yacht gave him a very generous check that more than helped the church become a reality.

I remembered that the Mass usually was scheduled to start at 9:30 AM, so quickly quaffing down a cup of coffee, I hopped into my Jeep and headed down the road to the settlement. The road up to the church wound along the side of the promontory-like hill ending it a parking lot, the church and a small modern rectory at its side. The church was ultramodern in design resembling the prow of a large boat with a cross, mounted over the apex of the arching roof.

I had arrived a few minutes early and took my place in one of the back pews. The musicians were setting up their instruments along the left side: an electric keyboard, drums and an electric guitar. The attendance at the Mass was usually limited to around fifty or sixty worshippers. I believe that the priest celebrated a Mass earlier on the other side of the island at one of the resorts.

The Mass began when a priest dressed in purple robes and accompanied by a cross bearer and two acolytes carrying candles processed up the center aisle. Behind him, entering the church late was my mysterious lady friend from the beach. She was wearing a form fitting white dress and a lace mantilla over her hair. She quickly took a seat in a pew on the other side of the church. I was amazed to see her under these circumstances.

The musicians started to sing "Amazing Grace" to a tempo that was more in tune to a rock concert performance. The priest was a tall black man with a goatee and mustache, most likely he was from the islands. His sermon went on and on for well over a half an hour. I kept glancing at the woman in the white dress, but she seemed to be focused on the words of the priest. After the Mass had ended, the musicians played another rousing hymn and the congregation started to leave the church. I exited quickly and waited outside in order to meet the woman before she was able to elude me.

After the last person had left the church, the usher closed the doors. Where was my mysterious lady? Was she still praying in the church? I opened the door and entered to find that the church was empty, except for two of the musicians who were packing away their instruments. Where did she go? I thought to myself. She just couldn't have disappeared into thin air. As I was leaving the church, the priest was locking the door to the rear sacristy. He turned and smiled at me.

"Are you enjoying your holiday on the island?" he asked me.

"Yes, Father, but I was wondering about a woman I saw attending the Mass this morning. She was dressed in white and was wearing a white mantilla over her hair. I saw her enter the church late, but after waiting outside for her to leave, I found that she didn't. In fact, she seemed to have disappeared. Is there another exit that she may have used?"

"Do you know this woman?" he asked me somewhat suspiciously.

"I met her on the beach the other day and didn't have a chance to find where she was living on the island?"

"I do not remember such a woman at Mass today. Our congregation is fairly small and any tourists attending Mass usually become quickly apparent to me," he said as he turned and locked the door to the church. "Perhaps you are mistaken. I would have remembered such a woman."

I walked back to my Jeep and sat behind the wheel. Am I hallucinating? I knew that I saw her. She was sitting in the back pew on the right side of the church. Is she just a figment of my imagination, I thought? After starting the Jeep and putting it in gear I drove down the narrow roadway that hugged the side of the steep hill and decided to drive back to my cottage at Guavaberry for some breakfast.

VII

It was a beautiful Sunday morning. After two cups of coffee and a thick slice of banana bread, I decided to take a walk down to Devil's Bay. I hadn't been there since I last trekked down to that isolated beach with Annie's brother, Tony Griffin. We found a great place that was off the wayward path where we could do some snorkeling sans our trunks. I found a real soul mate in Tony. Although he was ten years my junior, he became a great drinking buddy every time he came down to the islands with us. Whenever I couldn't find someone to go skinny-dipping, I didn't have to look further than my trim, muscular brother-in law. So I put on my white trunks, grabbed my snorkeling gear and dive bag and headed down the road toward the Baths.

The pathway to Devil's Bay veered left about ten meters from the traffic circle in front of The Top of the Baths. The path meandered for a quarter of a mile between and among the large granite boulders that marked the south end of the island. It was down hill all the way. When I finally reached my destination I found the place to myself. It didn't take me long to apply a coat of sunscreen over myself, especially being careful to coat my buns, since I would be hitting the water in the buff. It was a beautiful sunny late Sunday morning. Again I found myself wishing that Tony and Annie could be with me to enjoy the beautiful day.

As I stepped into the warm, crystal clear water, I sensed that I was not alone on the beach. The beach appeared totally deserted. Once in the water though, I swam out about twenty meters and immediately came across the impressive sight of three large tarpon. They must have been at least four foot long. I swam further across the bay being careful that I didn't leave the protective inner area for there was a strong current further out. I didn't want to be swept out to sea since I wasn't the strongest of swimmers.

I began to follow a good-sized sea turtle near the bottom of the bay in about twenty feet of water. After about ten minutes, I lost track of where I was, when I felt something touch the back of my right leg. I surfaced quickly to find that indeed my initial senses telling me that I was not alone proved to be correct. Facing me was my mysterious lady wearing a smile and nothing else.

I could feel myself becoming aroused at her sight. She was truly a beautiful woman. Slipping the snorkel from my mouth I asked her, "How did you find me here?"

"This is one of my favorite places to swim on the island. How did you know to come here today?" She laughingly asked me as she put her arms around me and pushed my head under the water.

I came up gasping for breath for her move had caught me off guard. After I cleared my facemask and took a deep breath, I questioned her.

"Weren't you the lady in white I saw in church this morning?"

She smiled coyly at me. "Yes, I love to listen to the wonderful music that is sung at St. Ursula's."

"Didn't you see there? I waited for you afterward but you seemed to have disappeared."

"I knew you'd be there, Danny."

She swam close to me and kissed me on the lips. Then she pushed herself away from me and began to swim toward the entrance of the bay. I almost threw care to the wind and followed her, but I knew that she would quickly be caught up in the strong tidal currents and swept beyond the point. I feared for her and my own safety. Was she trying to have me follow her where I might possibly be swept to sea and drown?

I called after her to return, but she soon disappeared around a rocky headland. I swam back to the beach where I had left my swim trunks and beach bag. I began to worry for her safety. She appeared to be a strong swimmer. Most likely she had left her towel and suit on a nearby beach. All I could think about was that she might be trying to do me harm by tempting me with these sexual escapades. I had to discover the identity of this woman. She had told me her name was Tess, yet, I knew not her last name.

I decided to approach the customs officials at the immigration building near the Virgin Gorda dock. Surely they would have a record of her arrival on the island.

VIII

After I had quickly showered and changed into a pair of walking shorts and a tropical print cotton shirt, I drove into the settlement with the intent of speaking to one of the immigration officers and also catch a quick lunch at the Bath and Turtle, a British style pub, located in the courtyard of the small shopping center in the yacht harbor. I ordered their flying fish sandwich and a pint of ale and sat watching the shoppers come and go in the center. Since it was Sunday, the bank and apothecary shops were closed for the day, but the rest of the businesses, including the gift and dive shops were open. I could see that the laundromat appeared to be busy with several people washing and drying their laundry.

A perky waitress served my lunch in record time. As I began to eat my lunch, I felt something rubbing against my right leg. I looked down under the table to find Sandy gazing up at me with her bright greenish brown eyes.

"What are you doing here girl?" I said as I petted her head. I reached over to my plate and offered her one of the French fries, which she quickly consumed. "You certainly have the run of the island. I'm heading back to Guavaberry. Do you need a ride back?"

She barked as if to tell me that she would like to ride back with me. Finishing my lunch I rose and headed back to my car with Sandy by my side.

I had forgotten to check with the custom official about the identity of my mystery lady. My thoughts were taken up with my new canine friend who sat next to me in the Jeep.

IX

I had the rest of the day free, so I decided to work on my manuscript. My narrative had reached the point where Annie, Griffin and I were beginning a new life on the Outer Banks of North Carolina.

When we finally arrived at the Duke Lab, we discovered the intense heat and humidity of the summer Carolina coast. We quickly realized that the staff and students at the lab adapt by dressing down, mainly in shorts, tee shirts and swimsuits. I checked into the main office and touched base with the director's administrative assistant, Gayle Willis. She welcomed me to the labs, gave me a set of keys to our apartment in the town of Beaufort and told me that there would be a reception for new people the following evening.

"The apartment is located in a complex of an old townhouse right on Front Street. There's parking for your car in the rear. All you have to do is move in. You'll find that it's completely furnished, even your bed linen and towels," she told me. After giving me directions to the apartment complex, I returned to the air-conditioned car and drove up across the lift bridge that led into the town of Beaufort. After we parked our car in the graveled driveway, we found that our home for the next two years would be in an early nineteen-century two story, white wooden framed house. We apparently had the apartment on the first floor. I prayed that the apartment was air-conditioned. Upon unlocking the rear door, I was overcome by a wall of hot air. Apparently it was not air-conditioned. We moved in and began to open windows. I found several electric fans that I placed around the apartment that cooled the place down a few degrees. I went to the front door and opened it to find that the apartment faced the sound and that there was a cool breeze coming in off the sea. At least it hopefully would cool off during the evening.

Annie started to look around at the furnishings after she put Griffin in a crib set up in the main bedroom. "Well, we're living in the South, my Dear. I suppose that we can learn to adapt to some hot weather."

"I'm going to go into Morehead City. It's is just across the bridge over the Newport River. I'll try to locate a hardware store. We're in need an air conditioner, at least for the bedroom. I'm already drenched in sweat and we've only been here less than an hour. Let's take Griffin and go for a drive in our air conditioned car. At least we can find some respite from the heat."

It was the first window model air-conditioner I had ever bought. Beaufort was a far cry weather-wise from the Pacific Northwest, where a hot day might reach temperatures in the low eighties and air conditioners were a rarity. After placing the air-conditioner in the bedroom window and turning it on, the apartment finally became tolerable.

We also had to change our style of wardrobe. We had brought our Seattle clothing with us: long pants, long sleeve shirts, sweaters, and even suits and ties. The first night Griffin slept wearing only his diaper while Annie and I stripped to the buff and let the cool air from the window air-conditioner soothe our naked bodies. Needless to say we took advantage of the opportunity to make love, however, we were both soaking wet by the time we had reached climax. We decided to check out the shower to cool off and found an old tub with a showerhead above it encircled by a shower curtain.

"Well, at least we have a shower," said Annie as we stepped into the tub, turned on the cooling water and made love one last time that night.

By the following morning, a front had moved through the area bringing with it some rain and cooler weather. I told Annie that I would have to go back to the lab and check out my research facilities. She decided that she would take Griffin out on a stroller tour of the town of Beaufort while I was gone.

The summer seemed to pass quickly. Before too long it was September and the weather took a turn for the better, with mild days that resembled the central coast of California. My research project on the developmental endocrinology of the blue crab was progressing at a good rate. Annie got involved with some of the Beaufort community activities with tag-a-long Griffin bringing up the rear.

On some weekends we ended up exploring the Outer Banks. Our first trip was out to Okracoke Island. We drove up to Cedar Island and boarded a ferry to the island, crossing Pamlico Sound. It brought back pleasant memories when we were dependent on ferries to transport us around the San Juan Islands. We spent the night on the island at an inexpensive motel after having a wonderful dinner at one of the local seafood restaurants. Then, early in the morning we headed north, up to Hatteras Island, where we connected with another ferry that took us across an inlet to the rest of the Sea Islands. Before long we were in the midst of the commercial center of the Outer Banks, Nags Head. While there we wandered up and down the beaches. Griffin got to splash in the surf and collected several seashells that he found on the beach.

One weekend, we headed south on US 17 and ended up driving all the way to Charleston, South Carolina. I had always wanted to visit the famous city where the American Civil War had begun. We spent the night at an old fashioned, Victorian bed and breakfast right in the historic district. The following morning we took a horse drawn carriage tour of the city. Griffin was most excited by the white "horsey."

When we returned to Beaufort, I discovered a letter from my former advisor at Washington. He received word that a tenured position for an invertebrate biologist had just opened at Bucknell University in Lewisburg, Pennsylvania. He told me that it was tailor made for me so I should make an application immediately. After asking for letters from my professors at Berkeley and Seattle and sending a resume of my research interests and an up to date vitae, I received a telephone call a week later from the chairman of the biology department to come up to Pennsylvania and interview for the position.

I discussed the situation with the director of the Duke Lab and he urged me to take the position, if it were to be offered to me. After all, he said, you can't turn down a golden opportunity to interview for a tenure track position.

"Your research here has shown promise," he told me. "The welcome mat will always be out for you at the Duke Lab, if you wish to return when your classes are not in session."

His support of my research did wonders for my ego. In fact, we did return the following summer when I did complete the project. This time the lab housed us in a new modern complex of air-conditioned apartments, a welcome change from when we first came to live and work at the Duke Lab.

I decided to drive up to Lewisburg taking Annie and Griffin with me, since I wanted her impressions of the school and the job position that was eventually offered to me.

The college, in the late sixties, resembled one of those Ivy League schools that comes to mind when one thinks of an eastern college. It was beautifully designed, with buildings laid out in a relatively symmetrical pattern. The architectural style was red Georgian brick with white porticos. A new chapel had just been built and dedicated a few years earlier and it served as the fulcrum of the entire campus.

I discovered that the chairman of the biology department, Fred Snyder, was a good friend to many of my college professors, both at Berkeley and Washington. Somehow I felt that I had an inside track in being considered for the position. My seminar was well received and I also found the biology staff of seven faculty members to be open to any of my questions. I knew that I would have no trouble becoming one of their colleagues.

Annie fell in love with the campus and the town of Lewisburg. "It will be a good place to raise our family," she told me as we were heading back south in our car to North Carolina.

A week after our return to the Duke Laboratory, I received a telephone call from the chairman offering me the position which would start the following September. Thus I had the rest of the year to complete my research project at the laboratory.

That night the director of the lab hosted a dinner party in my honor at his home. We celebrated my good fortune in finding a tenure-track position at a time when the job market for such positions was very tight.

Needless to say, I accepted the position thinking that it was a good place to get started. I initially intended to remain at the college for a few years and then begin to seek a position at a university like Duke that was affiliated with a marine laboratory where I would have the opportunity to carry out my blue crab research project. However, the few years turned into thirty-three. I eventually retired five years ago satisfied that I had had a successful career both in teaching my courses and carrying out a productive research program.

I had been working at the word processor for well over three hours. My thoughts returned to the mysterious woman who had captivated me. Where was she? I had to find out more about her.

X

Several more days had passed since I had arrived for my holiday in the British Virgin Islands. A new morning was dawning. It was the first morning that I could not remember dreaming about Annie during the night. I went into the bathroom and took my medication. I'd been somewhat remiss in forgetting to take my twice-daily regimen of capsules and pills. After a quick breakfast, I put on my swim trunks and a tee shirt and headed back down to Spring Bay for a morning swim. I harbored mixed emotions about whether or not I was hoping to meet my mysterious lady at the beach. When I arrived I found the beach empty of people. Again I had it to myself, so I stripped down and ran headlong into the sea. Either the water was warming up or I was used to the cooler spring temperature of the sea. It felt marvelous. I again began to swim laps. After twenty minutes I began to tire and decided to haul myself out of the water and sun-dry myself on one of the large flat rocks that bordered the beach.

After a few minutes I thought I heard voices coming down the path to the beach so I quickly grabbed my towel and trunks and made myself presentable to whomever was approaching. A party of two adults and three young children joined me on the beach. I was hoping that she might return. After waiting another half an hour, alas, my mystery lady did not appear.

As I was heading back to my cottage, I stopped at the Guavaberry office to visit Tina and her husband. After we exchanged pleasantries, Tina asked me if I would be interested in accompanying them to dinner that evening on the other side of the island.

"You really would enjoy visiting some of the resorts there," they told me. I didn't have the heart to tell them that I had been both to the Saba Rock Resort and The Bitter End Resort for dinner on more than one occasion with my family. However I thought that it would be a wonderful opportunity to return and relive fond memories of past visits.

"Ludwig will drive us to the ferry dock. I've asked Valerie to accompany us as well, so she will have an escort for the evening," she said. "We'll be up to Lily to pick you up around six o'clock."

"I'll see you then," I told them as I headed up the hill to my cottage.

Since we were going to one of the classier resorts, I decided to dress up a bit by putting on my white linen trousers and a colorful cotton shirt that had been silk screened with a pattern of tropical seashells. Annie had bought it for my birthday several years past in a print shop in Cruz Bay, St. John.

Tina and Ludwig, accompanied by Valerie, arrived at the stroke of six o'clock. I squeezed my large frame into their small Mitsubishi sedan and we began our trek to the other end of the island. There were several resorts at the north end of the island that were only accessible by boat. So after Ludwig skillfully navigated the small car up and over some precipitously steep mountain roads, missing most of the large potholes in the macadam coated highway, we finally made our way to North Sound where we parked the car and caught a small motor launch that took us across the inlet to the Saba Rock Resort.

As we approached the resort's dock, we were passed by another small passenger boat that was returning from the resort to the dock we had just left. I was surprised to catch the familiar face of my mystery lady sitting forward in the boat, dressed in a tight fitting green dress. When she caught sight of me, she smiled and waved her hand in greeting. Apparently I had just missed meeting her at the resort. Alas, all I could do was to return her greeting as the boats passed each other going in opposite directions.

Tina noticed that I had waved at the passing boat. I told her that there was a woman on the boat that I had met a few days before.

She looked at me strangely and replied that she missed seeing her on the boat.

I was perplexed. How could I have mistaken actually seeing her on that boat? Was my mind playing tricks on me?

When the boat docked at the resort, I asked the maitre 'd if anyone answering to her description had been at the resort.

No one remembered anyone that answered to her description as being at the resort that evening.

I started to question my sanity. Had I actually seen her on that boat that passed us on the way to the resort? Tina told me that she could have been leaving the Bitter End Resort.

I tried to make the most of the evening, but somehow I felt disappointed that I was unable to catch sight of her, or discover where she was living on the island.

XI

By the time Ludwig dropped me off at my cottage, I was dead tired. It had been a long and upsetting day. Even the dinner at the resort didn't sit well with me. I had picked through my food. I guess the three rum punches I had drunk with my food weren't helping my digestion. After visiting the bathroom, I undressed, turned out the lights and crawled into bed.

I was back in North Carolina, walking down one of the Outer Banks beaches with Annie by my side. Our son, Griffin, was running ahead of us, stopping now and then to pick up a shell that he put in a tin pail that he carried in his left hand. Annie looked up at me and smiled. It was a beautiful, warm sunny afternoon, a perfect day for a beachcombing walk.

"I'm glad that we came out here today, Dan darling. We only have so much time to spend with Griffin before he will be leaving us," she said as she squeezed my hand.

"Oh, I think Griffin will be with us for many more years. It'll be some years yet before he leaves us for college," I replied

as I glanced up the beach to find that Griffin was no longer in my sight.

"See, I knew that some day he would leave us," she said as she began to run up the beach in search of her son.

"Don't leave me too, Annie. He's probably hiding behind one of the sand dunes, playing one of his old tricks of hide and seek," I said.

"No, I think that the sea has taken him," said Annie. Yet her voice did not seem to show any sign of concern.

I started to take off my clothes and ran into the pounding surf at the edge of the beach, calling out his name as I went.

"Don't leave me, Danny. I'm afraid that that the sea will get me to. Come back to me. Griffin is a good swimmer. He'll make it back to us."

"I can't let him go. He'll drown for sure. He's not even two years old."

Annie started to run after me. The figure of a man that, in some way resembled our son, Griffin, was at her side. But instead of a young child, he appeared as a young adult, dressed in a suit and tie.

"See, here he is. Come out of the water before you drown," she ordered me.

"That man, who is holding your hand isn't our son. Can't you see that he isn't Griffin? He went into the sea. I'm sure of it."

"I have to leave with Griffin, darling. Please come out of the sea. I know that you'll drown if you don't."

"Please don't leave me, Annie. I'm sorry that you died. I love you so much. Please don't leave me again," I cried out to her as she and the young man who I had mistaken for my son suddenly disappeared from the beach.

I crawled on my hands and knees out of the sea and lay back on the wet sand. I found myself to be naked. It was night and I became chilled by the cold wind off the sea. I looked around and realized that I was no longer in North Carolina but on one of the strange turbulent beaches of the open Caribbean Sea. I stood up and began to run down the dark beach, stumbling as I ran, calling out Annie's name.

I awoke from my nightmare; my body drenched in sweat. Although the sun had yet risen, the feral roosters that freely roamed the Guavaberry grounds were beginning their early morning cacophony. I walked into the bathroom, turned on the shower and let the hot water pour over my body, for I was chilled to the bone even though my body was wet with sweat. Then I realized that my body reeked from the briny odor of seawater. I started to shake as fear overcame me. Had I been dreaming, or was I really transported to that far away beach with my departed wife?

XII

Later that morning, an hour after sunrise, I had taken my regimen of prescription drugs and went for a run down the road that led to the Baths. I felt that I had to clear my mind. When I was much younger and more able, I regularly ran two miles each morning. My illness, two years past, stopped me from running for a few months, but I decided that I had to return to my old regimen and gradually began to walk, then jog and finally run for at least for twenty minutes, three times a week. I had not done any real running, except for swimming, as my only form of exertion since I arrived on the island. By the time I reached the path down to the Baths, I was sweating profusely, yet I felt somewhat cleansed of my nocturnal experience.

On my way to my cottage, I stopped at the Guavaberry office. I had decided to call my son, Grif. Even though there was a four-hour time difference between island time and the U.S. West Coast, I felt that my "so-called dream" was in fact an ill omen that in someway may indicate a potential danger to my son.

Of course, the phone call roused him from a sound sleep. At first he was upset, but discovering the call was from his father seemed to mollify his irritated state.

"What's up, Pop? Why the early morning call?"

"I'm down in the islands visiting Virgin Gorda on my own. I just wanted to touch base with you," I said trying to sound non-chalant.

"Well, I was about to get up anyway. Some of my friends have scheduled an early morning SCUBA dive off the Farallones and they talked me into going along with them."

I couldn't shake the feeling that something might happen to him, if he continued on with such a venture.

"When was the last time you did any diving, Grif?

"Oh, it's been a couple of years. But most of my diving has been limited to the Caribbean. This would be a first for me. I had to rent a quarter inch wet suit to wear, other wise I'd freeze my balls off."

"What does your wife, Sophie, think of your going out diving in the Pacific?"

"She tried to talk me out of it," he said. "She's always concerned about me diving, even when I dived in the Caribbean."

"Would you do me a favor, Grif, and heed her concerns. I had a dream last night that you went into the sea and didn't return."

"Wow! Now you're creeping me out too. I already paid several hundred bucks to go along with the group. They'd think I was a pansy if I tried to duck out of going."

"How do you feel about going, Grif?" I asked him. "Diving the Farallones would be a very strenuous and challenging experience for you. And it's been a few years since you've done any diving."

"Look, Pop, if it makes you and Sophie feel any better, I'll be certain to take it easy. The first rule of diving is you don't get yourself into a situation that you are uncomfortable with. If it looks like there's any danger involved with the dive, I'll play the pansy and stay near the surface. The guys are going down looking for abalone, something I don't feel like doing anyway since I don't like the taste of snails."

I started to feel foolish, alarming my son about a dream that I had experienced. Yet I couldn't discount the feeling so ominous that I just couldn't sit back and do nothing about it. Griffin had always been the one to throw care to the wind. I remembered the time he had gone skiing with some college friends up in the Sierras in an area that was well known to be prone to avalanches. Fortunately, his ski trip was without any such incidence.

After I had told him to take it easy with the dive and that I loved him, I headed back to my cottage. On my return I found my new friend Sandy waiting for me at in front of the cottage door.

"Well, welcome back, girl. Where'd you go last night?

She looked up with a wistful look. "Let me take a quick shower. Wait for me and I'll give you a ride in the Jeep. I have to go to the settlement and run some errands."

After I showered and changed into some clean clothes, I returned to the deck to find that Sandy was no where to be seen.

XIII

I stopped at the Bath and Turtle and ordered Mount Gay rum on the rocks to steady my rattled nerves. While I was nursing my drink at the bar, I struck up a conversation with the barkeep. I asked him if he had ever seen an attractive woman with golden blond hair. I tried to describe her to him to the best of my ability.

"There are a lot of attractive women that come to the island," he responded as he started to wipe the top of the bar with a damp cloth. Do you have a picture of her?"

"Unfortunately, I do not," I said as I finished my drink and left the pub.

I stopped off at Buck's to pick up some provisions and headed back to my car.

On the drive back to my cottage at Guavaberry, I decided to stop at the office and phone my son, Grif. I was still concerned about the dream I had experienced that night. When the phone rang, I was surprised that Grif answered my call.

"I thought you were going diving with some friends this morning?" I asked him.

"Pop, your call this morning really spooked me. I decided at the last minute to cancel out on the trip. It turns out that your call saved my life. On the way to the Farallon Islands, the dive boat called in an SOS to the Coast Guard that they were sinking after the boat's engine caught fire. I haven't heard the final word, but by the time the Coast Guard got to the disabled boat, it had already sunk and they were pulling survivors out of the sea. I'm watching the cable television news coverage at the moment. It looks like all the divers save one were rescued."

Did I have a premonition that something could have happened to my son? I was starting to sense that something was happening to me.

In another week or so I would be joined at Guavaberry by my daughter Marty and her husband, Bruce. They promised to keep me from getting too lonely. Far from it, I thought to myself. It had been days since I had been working on my book. I had this freaky feeling that I was about to become involved in what could possibly be dangerous.

XIV

I had stopped writing my book for the time being. My preoccupation with the mystery woman was definitely interfering with my ability to concentrate on my writing. I could not get her out of my mind. Where was she today? I had not caught sight of her for more than a day. She was starting to possess my thoughts.

Luck was with me when I finally was able to contact the harbormaster, a tall, gaunt looking fellow with a salt and pepper beard and mustache. He introduced himself to me as Craig Goodbody. He told me that a woman matching my description was seen in the company of one of the men who moored his yacht in a slip in the yacht basin.

"Perhaps, you can touch base with him today. He may either be on his boat or be at the marina picking up provisions."

I thanked him for the information and began to walk down the floating pier to find a sleek fiberglass hulled sloop in a slip near the end of the dock. On the foredeck, I found a young fellow, in his mid-thirties, who was washing down the deck of his boat. He was dressed in a pair of red Speedo briefs that allowed him to display his well-tanned muscular torso and his large "endowment."

I called out to him and introduced myself. "I'm told that you know of a woman with light blond hair whom I am interested in contacting. She told me her name was Tess," He looked at me quizzically and said, "Why do you want to find this woman? What interest do you have in her?"

"I met her last week on the beach at Guavaberry," although I hated to lie to him, I said, "She was wearing a ring that I later found on the beach. It appears to be an expensive piece of jewelry. I'd just like to return it to her."

"The only blond I know lives in a beach house across from "The Bitter End Resort" on the north end of the island. The only thing, though she don't go by the name of Tess. She's quite a looker though. I took her out on a cruise once and before I knew it, she was in the buff, asking me to help her apply suntan lotion to her body. I must admit, by the time I had finished I had a roaring heart on and had stripped down and was making out with her right on the deck. We nearly ran aground, but that fuck was more than worth it."

I tried not to show any interest in his crude story, but I felt that his sex partner may be one and the same as the woman who called herself Tess. "Is there any way that I could touch base with her? I'd like to return her diamond ring."

"Ain't no sea taxis around here, but if you charter my boat for the day. I'll run you over for a hundred bucks. I know where her beach house is located. There is a rutted road to the house, but it's badly in need of repair. Best way to access it is by boat. Oh, by the way, my name is Andy, Andy Stepford. I supplement my income by chartering out my boat, "The Wet Willy" for excursion and diving around the island."

"How's about taking me out tomorrow morning?"

"Got nothing on my log for tomorrow. Be here bright and early, say 0700 hours and we'll cruise over to the other end of the island and check her out. You might get lucky for returning her ring."

"I'll be here on time," I replied to his crude remark.

"Be in time for breakfast. I like to whip up some eggs and bacon. It keeps me going for the rest of the morning."

"Sounds like a good deal," I replied as I headed back to my parked car in the marina. I made a quick stop at the marina market, for I was running low on provisions.

XV

I awoke early the next day with a severe headache. I realized that I forgot to take my prescription drugs the night before. I stumbled into the bathroom that put me in touch with the pills that I downed quickly with a glass of water then, I hiked down to Spring Bay for a quick swim. By the time I reached the beach, I was aware that dark storm clouds were appearing on the southeast horizon. Apparently a squall line would bring rainstorms that would soon be upon me. By the time I finished my swim, a gusty wind had come up, bringing with it a train of waves that were breaking onto the beach. I began to wonder if Andy would be canceling our trip to the other end of the island. Since I didn't have any way of contacting him, I would just have to drive over to the marina to find out if it was a "go" for today

After hiking back to my cottage, since Andy promised to treat me to breakfast, I decided to brew myself a cup of hot tea. After a quick rinse off in the shower, I dressed for inclement weather with my deck shoes, a pair of jeans and a red windbreaker over my white polo shirt. When

I stepped out onto the deck, I saw no sign of my canine friend. I began to wonder where she had gone. I was starting to miss being greeted by her in the morning.

By the time I drove to the marina, the squall line had hit the yacht harbor. I waited in my jeep until the heavy rain had somewhat abated and then made a quick dash for Andy's dock.

Arriving at his boat, my sense of smell was greeted by the aroma of frying bacon and fresh brewed coffee. I stepped onto the deck of the boat holding on to one of the sail's cable lines. I called out to him, "Ahoy, Andy! Where you be?"

"I'm below in my galley, whipping up some grub for breakfast. C'mon down. Be careful, though, the steps are wet from the rain."

I slowly descended down the slippery wooden steps to find him busily cooking in the small galley at a two-burner butane stove. I was taken aback to find him naked except for a canvas apron around his midsection that barely covered his genitals. All he wore was a pair of scuffed white deck shoes and a heavy gold chain around his neck.

"Hope you don't find me a bit weird, but I rarely wear anything when I'm below. It gets too damned hot down here since I don't have air conditioning on board," he said as he turned and handed me a tall glass of tomato juice. "When I'm entertaining lady friends, I usually start by wearing a sarong, but I usually am able to talk most of the gals into joining me in the buff," he started to laugh, as he reached down with his cooking spatula and scratched his privates.

I began to feel a bit awkward being in his presence, though I was aware that the air in the small galley was hot and very humid. I took a drink of the juice to find that it was heavily spiked with vodka and a spicy hot sauce.

"Hope you like my own special concoction of a Bloody Mary. I usually have one before I set sail and cast off, but I only drink near beer when I am under sail, although I have plenty more where that came from, if you'd like to have another."

I came to realize that I was about to sail with one of the more colorful island characters. "Just one of these will do me just fine," I told him, as I sat down at the small galley table.

He soon set a tin plate loaded with scrambled eggs and a rasher of crisp bacon before me. "The coffee is just about ready. How do you take it?" he said, as he set a bowl of fresh fruit and a tray of buttered toast before me.

"Just black will do me fine," I replied as I began to dig into the hearty breakfast that he had set before me.

He quickly sat down across from me placing another plate of food on the table.

As he turned to sit, I couldn't help but notice that he displayed a nasty looking scar that ran from his navel, down his belly into his hairy pubic region. "A battle scar from one of your more amorous lady friends?" I asked him as I looked down at his muscular torso.

"Only time I wish I had been wearing a wet suit," he said as he ran the fingers of his right hand down the scar. "I used to snorkel in the raw whenever I took a party out diving. I didn't run into any problems talking my guests into joining me for a dip in the raw, but one afternoon I got caught up in a swell when I was swimming across a shallow reef. I was dragged across some sharp reef coral that almost gutted me and nearly cut my cock off. I lucked out. One of my guests on board was a doctor who was able to stitch me up. Otherwise I most likely would have chucked it there and then. That taught me a lesson to steer clear of snorkeling in the raw across shallow reefs. I now wear a shorty wet suit when I dive on shoreline reefs. It keeps me from having a repeat of that day, if I have to take my guests into such dangerous areas."

As I was finishing my second cup of hot coffee and sweating profusely, he asked me if he could see the ring I was supposed to have found on the beach.

Damn, I swore to myself, I was caught in a lie. "I didn't find a ring. I'm just interest in meeting her. She nearly made out with me while we swam at Spring Bay."

I stuck my right hand into the pocket of my windbreaker and pulled out a ring. Now how did that get in there, I thought? Had she come to my cottage while I was asleep and left it as a souvenir for me to find. Checking the ring more closely, I realized that it was the same ring that Tess had been wearing. Suddenly I realized that I held in my hand my wife's sapphire and diamond engagement ring that I had given to her over forty years ago. I thought that I gave it to Marty the year after Annie had died. How could it be the same ring? I began to realize that somehow she was trying to communicate with me.

"Thought you said you didn't have the ring, but I can't blame you. She's quite a piece and that's quite a nice ring," he started to laugh. "I don't know if she's the same woman you've described to me," he replied as he took a drink from his coffee cup. Changing the subject, he said, "Well, we'll be ready to set sail in about an hour. I want to wait until the squall line moves through. We'll sail up the west coast of Gorda. It should be smoother, plus we'll have the winds in our favor, won't have to tack as much until we reach the north side of the island."

I put the ring back into my pocket. My mind was in turmoil. Did Marty slip the ring into my coat before she took me to the airport? That had to be the answer. Such rings don't just magically appear.

An hour later, although there was still a moderate wind from the east, Andy decided to cast off after we had finished breakfast. He pulled on a pair of tight white shorts and a yellow polo shirt. I was relieved that I would not have to sail with him while he was butt naked.

Andy started up the engine that we used to sail up the west coast of Virgin Gorda, past the resort at Little Dix Bay. When we reached Savanna Bay, we picked up a breeze that was coming from the west. At that point he cut the engine and I helped him set the main sail, which quickly caught the wind.

"We're in luck," said Andy. "We should arrive at our destination sooner than I thought, probably thirty or forty minutes. Her beach house is not at North Sound, but on Leverick Bay. I haven't been to the house, but she told me it's painted a bright yellow with a red tile roof. Should be easy to spot."

As we rounded the northwest point of the island, the wind started to come from the east. Andy began to tack his boat in a zig-zag direction. I was forced to help him adjust the boom of the mainsail as we began to tack against the wind.

We finally entered Leverick Bay where he furled the mainsail and began to power the boat with his main engine. There were several houses built along the cove like bay. Which one was hers, I thought.

"There it is, to the right, the one with the red tile roof," shouted Andy over the loud roaring of the boat's engine. Fortunately we were able to moor the boat at a small wooden dock that extended out from the rocky shoreline. Since ours was the only boat at the dock, I began to wonder if anyone would be home at the beach house.

"She's probably here," said Andy almost reading my thoughts. "I see her red Jeep parked along side the house. She's quite adept at driving on what's left of the access road that splits off the main highway over Gorda peak."

The house was built into the rocky cliff face that dropped steeply to the shoreline. A staircase of weathered wood extended from the dock to a deck that overlooked the sea. We made our way up the stairs to find the deck filled with ornate wrought iron furniture. A wooden trellis against the sidewall of the house was overgrown with an iridescent red bougainvillea in full bloom that added a spectacular touch to the otherwise plain deck.

Andy walked over to the front double doors that were painted a bright red. Although the doors were partially ajar, he reached for the brass knocker and rapped on the doors three times.

"I think she should be home since her car is here," said Andy, as he turned and looked out at the spectacular view of Leverick Bay and Mosquito Island in the distance.

After a wait of several minutes, no one had yet to answer the knock on the door. He rapped on the door again. This time, the door started to open revealing a well-appointed hallway that led to a great room, beautifully furnished with overstuffed wicker furniture and a massive open circular stone fireplace in the center of the room.

I was hesitant to enter into the house, but he insisted that we look for his friend.

"She might be out back, or perhaps she's taking a nap," he said. I felt that we were definitely trespassing. Andy walked into the adjoining kitchen, that, like the large living room was well appointed with the state of the art kitchen appliances.

"Hey, Girl!" Andy called out. "Where the hell are you?" No answer. His voice reverberated through the house.

"I don't think she's home, Andy," I said. I was beginning to become uncomfortable wandering around a stranger's home.

"Let's look around outside. She may be working on her garden."

We walked through the kitchen. I noticed a half filled cup of coffee on the table in the breakfast nook. Upon opening the glass doors, we found a large wooden deck that contained a large collection of potted orchids, most of which were in full bloom. I suddenly became aware of a fetid smell in the air that grew stronger as we rounded the curved wooden deck.

"Oh, Christ sake!" exclaimed Andy as we first caught sight of a decomposing body of what appeared to be the remains of a woman. Her body appeared to be naked. Her skin had turned a dark brown. She apparently had been dead for some time from the amount of decomposition and the strong fetid smell arising from her body. Andy turned and started to wretch and vomited over the deck guard railing.

Although my stomach was turning flip-flops, I could not turn my eyes away from the decaying corpse. Although her hair was golden in color, the roots were dark gray. Could this have been the woman that had been tempting me? I became aware on closer inspection that her neck had been slashed. A dark hardened pool of blood covered the deck beneath her body. I realized then that she had been apparently killed….murdered!

"We've got to report this to the island police," I said to Andy, who was wiping his mouth on his shirt sleeve.

"I don't want to get involved with this," he said. "Let's get the hell out of here. Nobody's seen us sail up to her dock. I can't afford a run in with the police."

"We just can't leave her like this, after all she was a human being. And it looks like her death wasn't accidental, in fact it looks like she's been murdered," I said.

"We could always make an anonymous call to the police when we get back from one of the pay phones near the dock," he said as he turned and headed back into the house on his way to his docked boat.

I followed him being careful not to touch anything. I was concerned that if I left my fingerprints that I could be implicated in her death. Yet I felt guilty for it was the coward's way out to just leave her body lying there.

"Shouldn't we at least make a report in person to the island police?"

"No way. And I urge you to forget what you saw. We don't need the hassle of the police questioning us, especially me, since I've had a run in with her at a bar over at the Bitter End a few months ago. The last thing I need is to be a suspect in her murder."

I knew that I had to report the murder of the woman, even though Andy insisted that I should not. The return sail to the marina was spent in silence. I went on the upper deck and began to realize that we had passed the entrance to the marina . Turning I found Andy was standing behind me holding a wicked looking knife in his right hand.

"I can't trust you now with what you have seen," he said.

"What's going on?" I replied apprehensively.

"What do you think, old man? I can't let you live seeing what I did to that dame. She was blackmailing me, the bitch. I don't plan to rot away in no stinkin' island prison over that slut. I was planning to rob and kill you as well and leave your body next to hers, hoping that the police would implicate you in the murder. But then I had second thoughts and figured I could easily dispose of you at sea and not have to worry about either of you."

He lunged at me with the knife. I quickly sidestepped and grabbed at his hand, cutting my own hand with the sharp knife. We struggled for a few moments at the edge of the deck. Suddenly the wind shifted causing the boom of the main sail to knock both of us overboard. I started to sink and thought that I was going to drown. I looked up at the shimmering mirrored surface of the sea and realized it would be the last thing I would see. I began to lose consciousness. Suddenly I became aware of being lifted up by an arm around my chest that helped me break through the surface of the sea. I turned to find my mystery lady smiling at me.

"Take my arm," she told me. "We're not that far from reaching shore."

I looked over my shoulder to find that indeed we were just a hundred yards from a boulder covered island, just off the southeast tip of Virgin Gorda. Within a few minutes, I struggled ashore with her help. I couldn't help but notice that she was wearing a yellow and red bikini, in addition to a big smile on her beautiful face.

"I don't think that your friend was as lucky as you. I'm afraid that he couldn't out swim the strong current," she said as she held my right hand. "You have a nasty cut on your hand that needs caring. It's bleeding badly. Let me take part of your shirt and tie a tourniquet around it."

"Who are you?" I asked her. "You always appear unexpectedly, yet I can never find you on the island."

As she helped me off with my wet shirt and began to tear a strip from the tail, she smiled at me. "Don't you recognize me, Danny?"

I looked deeply into her eyes and suddenly realized that it was my Annie who was standing before me.

"Annie, Annie!" I cried out. "Is it really you? How can this be? You left me two years ago. Are you a ghost?" I reached out with my arms to embrace her and held her wet body in my arms. She kissed me passionately on the lips. It was her. It was her.

"You don't remember, do you, my darling. I promised you as I lay dying that I would come back to you when you returned to this beautiful island. The Good Lord granted me my wish, but He allowed me to appear to you in the form of an island dog, but I had the consciousness of my own former self. You named me Sandy. Yet I also was granted the ability to appear as a woman when you would eventually appear on the island. For the past two years I have been waiting for you, hoping that you would return to Hibiscus cottage, here at Guavaberry on Virgin Gorda. The night you invited Sandy into your cottage to sleep in your bed, I was able to leave my ring in your jacket as a symbol of my presence."

"Tell me this is all a dream. I'm going to wake up in my bed back at Guavaberry."

"It's not a dream, my darling. Look at your hand. Does the wound still bleed?"

I discovered that my hand showed no trace of any wound. I looked down at myself to find that my body appeared to have been transformed. I no longer possessed the body of a seventy year old man. My bare chest and arms were now tanned and muscular, and covered with the dark curly hair of my youth.

"In death the Good Lord has granted you a new body, the glorified body of a young man. You drowned today after you fell off the boat, my darling. You and I now can begin an eternity together," said Annie as she embraced me with her lithe arms of her own glorified body.

I realized that my consciousness was fully opened and I finally knew that I had been awarded a wonderful gift, the promised gift of eternal life that I now would share forever with my beloved Annie.

EPILOGUE

"Hello! Am I speaking to Mr. Griffin Henderson, the son of Professor Daniel Henderson?"

"Yes, it is. Who is calling please?"

My name is Tina Gottscheid. I'm calling from Virgin Gorda in the British Virgin Islands. I'm the manager of Guavaberry Spring Bay Vacation Homes. Your father has been a guest at our resort for the past few weeks. I'm afraid that I have to report some bad news about your father. Fortunately I was able to find your telephone number in the log we maintain by the phone our guests use in making long distance calls."

"What's wrong? What happened to him? Did he have an accident?" came the anxious voice of Griffin over the telephone.

"Two days ago he last was seen in the company of Andrew Stepford, the owner-captain of the sloop, The Wet Willie. He apparently had chartered the boat for a sail. Yesterday the boat was found capsized off the north end of the Peter Island. Your father and Captain Stepford were missing and presumed lost at sea. Today the body of

Stepford was found by a pleasure craft. It was floating in shallow water off Fallen Jerusalem, a small rocky island south of Virgin Gorda. The coastal authorities have assumed that your father has also drowned, though his body has yet to be found."

"Oh, my God!" cried Griffin. "Couldn't he still be alive? Is there a chance he was able to make it to shore on one of the islands? I can't believe this."

"I suppose there is still hope," said Tina to the distraught man. "But he has not shown up anywhere. There is a search underway to try to locate him or his remains."

"My father has spent many years in the islands teaching marine biology to his students. I can't believe that he just fell off a boat and drowned. He has to be somewhere. He has to be."

"Would you be able to book travel to Virgin Gorda? Perchance you could aid in the search for your father. He also has his possessions remaining in one of our cottages, including his personal laptop computer."

"I'll contact my sister in Pennsylvania. I believe she and her husband were to join him there in another week or so. I'll make arrangements to leave San Francisco as soon as I can schedule a flight to the islands. I think that she and I should be arriving there in a couple of days. Perhaps by then the authorities may be able to have more information about him."

"I hope that he is just missing and no harm has come to him," replied Tina. I'm sorry to be the bearer of such sad news. We look forward to seeing you here. Have a safe flight. Goodbye."

Two days later Grif, accompanied by his sister Marty and her husband, Bruce, arrived on the St. Thomas ferry to Virgin Gorda. Tina was there to greet them and pick them up with her small car.

"There's still no news to report about your father. I am sorry that he still is considered missing and presumed dead," said Tina to her visitors. "I'll take you up to Guavaberry. We've prepared accommodations for you in Hibiscus cottage."

"I still don't accept the fact that my father is dead," said Grif.

"He can't be dead," said Marty. "I can't believe that he'd go sailing with someone who he barely knew."

"Andy Stepford had an unsavory reputation on the island," said Tina. "I too can't believe that your father would go sailing with him, especially without checking on his reliability. A few days ago the body of a woman who was apparently murdered was discovered by her maid. She had a small villa up at Leverick Bay. The police have discovered evidence that implicates Mr. Stepford. The authorities are concerned that he may also be responsible for your father's disappearance."

"Would you mind allowing us to speak to someone in charge of this investigation?" asked Grif. "We'd like to find out if they have any news about our father?"

"I'll stop over at the police kiosk before driving to Guavaberry," replied Tina.

Arriving at the police station, they were informed that there was no new information concerning the disappearance of their father. Tina then drove the dejected family back to Guavaberry in silence. The car made its way through the front gate and into the resort complex.

"We've moved your father's belongings into Hibiscus cottage. It's a two bedroom unit that you should remember from your last visit to the island," said Tina as she parked her car in front of the cottage. "Your father and mother loved the view of the islands from the deck. I hope that you will find it suitable during your stay with us. Again, we offer our deepest condolences on the disappearance of your father. He had become a very special friend of our family."

"Thank you," said Marty as she and her husband removed the luggage and carried it up the steps to the upper deck.

"What cottage did my father rent while he was staying here?" asked Grif.

"He had rented Lily cottage, a one bedroom unit. You can see it to your right, just south of Hibiscus," replied Tina. "He was scheduled to move into Hibiscus when his daughter and her husband were to join him, in another week."

When they reached the deck they discovered two island dogs under the table. The dogs were sitting upright, their tails wagging in greeting.

"Looks like we have a welcoming committee at hand," laughed Grif. "Are they part of the Guavaberry family?" he asked Tina.

"I don't recognize them as belonging to the resort family," replied Tina. "They must belong to some other island family."

"They look like a mated pair," said Grif, as he reached down and stroked the head of the larger, gray coated male. "He seems very friendly, aren't you boy?"

"Come over here," said Grif to his sister, Marty, as he sat before his father's lap top computer which he had placed on the table on the deck. "I've been reading sections of Dad's new book about his life with Mom and us kids. Look at the forward. He dedicated the book to his children. That's us-you and me."

Marty came over to his side and looked at the monitor screen. "I knew that he had been working on this book for several months now. He told me that he was planning to finish writing the book while he was in the islands."

"Did he complete his story?" asked Bruce who was sitting in a canvas chair next to his wife.

Grif tabbed to the last page of the manuscript and began to read it.

I've been reminiscing about my life with Annie and my children. It's been wonderful to spend the last two weeks down here in the islands. The memories of the past years have invigorated me. I feel that Annie somehow has found a way to be with me.

I also have found a new companion in Sandy, an island dog that appears to have taken a liking to me, and I to her. There's something mysterious about, her, though. No one here appears to know where she came from. She just appeared on the deck of my cottage a day or so after I arrived. Even more mysterious was the appearance of a beautiful woman who I met on the beach the first day I went swimming at Spring

Bay. I must admit there was something about her that was attractive to me. Like the dog, no one seems to know who she was. We swam together on two occasions. I'm embarrassed to admit that she like I like to skinny dip. I feel guilty admitting that we came close to a relationship on one occasion. In certain ways she reminds me of my Annie.

Annie, my Darling Annie, I will always love you. Your spirit will always be with me. You are beyond remembrance.......

"That's Dad's last entry in the book's file. It appears to be dated two days before he went on that final sail with Stepford," said Grif as he closed down the file and logged off the computer.

Sitting between her brother and her husband, Bruce, Marty gazed out over the shimmering sea and the islands in the distance. "Somehow I feel that Dad is at peace. He found Mom down here. I think their spirits, buoyed up by the deep love they have always shared for each other, will always remain as part of these beautiful islands."

She reached over to her brother and took his hand in hers as they watched the two island dogs frolicking as they scampered down the road toward the beach.